THE WHISPERS ABOUT MY FATHER GREW STRONGER.

It was said that one group of men was planning to waylay Sequoyah with rifles and shoot him to death.

Finally, those who cared about Sequoyah decided that there was only one way to turn my father from his dangerous path. They made a plan to hide themselves in the woods near his cabin while Sally drew my father away.

"My husband," Sally told him, "come with me. There is something you must see."

When Sequoyah was far enough away, his concerned neighbors came out of the woods and went into the little building. They were shocked at what they saw. Those symbols that might be witchcraft were not just drawn on pieces of paper and chips of wood. They were scrawled on the walls, carved into the table and the chairs. Those brave enough to go into that cabin only stayed long enough in that frightening place to set it ablaze. Because it was filled with all those papers and dry chips of wood, it took almost no time at all before the roof collapsed as the flames roared up.

OTHER BOOKS
BY JOSEPH BRUCHAC

The Arrow over the Door

Children of the Longhouse

Code Talker

Eagle Song

The Heart of a Chief

Jim Thorpe, Original All-American

March Toward the Thunder

Wabi

The Winter People

Joseph Bruchac
TALKING LEAVES

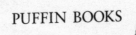

PUFFIN BOOKS

PUFFIN BOOKS
An imprint of Penguin Random House LLC
375 Hudson Street
New York, New York 10014

First published in the United States of America by Dial Books for Young Readers,
an imprint of Penguin Random House LLC, 2016
Published by Puffin Books, an imprint of Penguin Random House LLC, 2017

THE LIBRARY OF CONGRESS HAS CATALOGED THE DIAL BOOKS FOR YOUNG READERS EDITION AS FOLLOWS:
Names: Bruchac, Joseph, 1942–author.
Title: Talking leaves / by Joseph Bruchac.
Description: New York, NY : Dial Books for Young Readers, [2016] | Summary:
"The story of Sequoyah and the creation of the Cherokee syllabary, as told
by his thirteen year old son"—Provided by publisher.
Identifiers: LCCN 2015035887 | ISBN 9780803735088 (hardback)
Subjects: | CYAC: Sequoyah, 1770?–1843–Fiction. | Cherokee Indians—Fiction.
| Indians of North America—Fiction. | Language and languages—Fiction. |
BISAC: JUVENILE FICTION / People & Places / United States / Native
American. | JUVENILE FICTION / Historical / United States / 19th Century.
| JUVENILE FICTION / Family / Parents.
Classification: LCC PZ7.B82816 Tal 2016 | DDC [Fic]—dc23 LC record available at
http://lccn.loc.gov/2015035887

Puffin Books ISBN 9780142422984

Printed in the United States of America

1 3 5 7 9 10 8 6 4 2

Design by Nancy Leo-Kelly

To those,
past and present,
who have worked to preserve our native tongues

CHARACTERS

Main Characters:

Uwohali (Big Eagle):
Main character who tells the story,
son of Sequoyah by Sequoyah's first marriage

U-ti-yu:
Uwohali's mother who married Sequoyah in 1801,
then divorced him

Sequoyah:
Creator of the Cherokee syllabary, Uwohali's father.
Also known as George Guess.

Ahyokah (She Brought Happiness):
Sequoyah's six- or seven-year-old daughter who is
Uwohali's half sister

Sally Guess:
Sequoyah's second wife, who married him in 1815,
mother of Ahyokah

Secondary Characters:

Uwohali's Friends:

Yugi (Nail): his best, most loyal friend

Ugama (Soup)

Udagehi (Baby)

Gayusoli (Nose)

Galuloi (Sky)

Equgugu (Big Owl)

Uwohali's Three Uncles:

Red Bird

Blackbird (John)

White Raven (Samuel)

Agili (He Is Rising):
Village Chief of Willstown, where the story takes place.
Also known as George Lowrey

Charles Hicks:
friend of Sequoyah, son of a Cherokee woman
and a Scots trader

Turtle Fields: friend of Sequoyah

Big Rattling Gourd: friend of Sequoyah

Old Turkey: a stickball maker

Wuh-teh: Sequoyah's deceased mother

Black Fox: father of Equgugu

Gu-nun-da-le-gi:
One Who Follow the Ridge, Cherokee name of the man
who became known as "Major Ridge"

Oo-loo-deh-gah (John Jolly):
Chief of the Western Cherokees (Old Settlers) who
emigrated to Arkansas in 1807.

Tsunu'lahun'ski (or Junaluska):
famous past Cherokee chief

Golanu (the Raven):
the Cherokee name for Sam Houston, who they also
affectionately called "Big Drunk." Houston fought under
General Andrew Jackson at the Battle of Horseshoe Bend
and later was one of the founders of the Republic of Texas

Sharp Knife:
Cherokee name for General Andrew Jackson

Red Sticks:
Members of the Upper Creek Nation who tried to drive out
the whites and were eventually defeated by a coalition of
Lower Creeks, Cherokees, and white soldiers commanded
by General Andrew Jackson

TABLE

1. My Father Is Crazy   3

2. My Mother Is Worried   10

3. Sitting and Thinking   21

4. I Greet You, Young Man   36

5. Ahyokah's Friends   48

6. Marbles   56

7. The Chunkey Players   66

8. Confused Thoughts   79

9. At the Town House   84

10. My Mother Knows   99

11. An Uncertain Fish   104

12. Marks in the Clay   115

13. I Agree   123

14. Leaves That Talk   128

OF CONTENTS

15. Going to War   143

16. Horseshoe Bend   153

17. 86 Symbols   163

18. Yugi's Warning   170

19. Seeing the Sun Land   179

20. Learning   188

21. Footsteps   200

22. The Village Chief's Visit   212

23. Good or Bad   220

24. The Test   227

Afterword   237

Sequoyah's Cherokee Syllabary   239

Cherokee Words   240

Further Reading   242

Acknowledgments   244

WILLSTOWN, ALABAMA,

1821

CHAPTER 1

MY FATHER IS CRAZY

Crazy. That is the best thing they whisper about my father.

Black magic. Witchcraft. What he is doing or trying to do is evil medicine. That's the worst.

Since he returned from the West three weeks ago I have heard nothing but bad things said about him. Is it just those bad words that have kept me from going to see him? Am I afraid that when I do see him—if I see him—I will think he is crazy, too?

I am also uncertain how he will treat me if I show up at his door. Maybe he will not be glad to see me. Maybe he will tell me to go away. He has another child now, my half sister, Ahyokah. My father spends much of his time with her. She's his favorite, not me. I think he loved me once. I remember the stories he used to tell me in his gentle voice. But if he really cared about me, why did he leave me and go to Arkansas? Why have I never heard anything from him during the years he was gone from our town?

Others of our people who emigrated to those western places have sent messages by way of the traders and missionaries who are always moving back and forth between our people. Some, who have learned English, have even sent written letters. But not my father, Sequoyah. No word, either written or spoken, has ever come to me from him.

Maybe he has even forgotten that he ever had a son.

Still, despite all my uncertainty, I have almost gone to where he is living at the home of his second wife. Last week I walked halfway across town toward their cabin before I turned back and returned to my mother's cabin.

How long will my father be able to stay here? Some say that if it was not for the fact that Agili, who is now the chief of our town, was my father's cousin and oldest friend, he would have been forced to leave—or worse. I worry I will not get the chance to see him before he is driven away.

I tap the chunkey stick I am holding against the ground. The ground sounds hollow as I do so, almost like a drum. It still holds the cold of winter inside it, even though it will not be long until the leaves return.

I don't mind the cold. I know the song to keep frostbite away before going out to hunt for food when it is cold. It's the song that calls on the deer, whose feet cannot be hurt by frost or snow, to share that power with the hunter.

I start to sing it to the rhythm of my stick striking the ground.

> *Tusunkawiye. Tusunkawiye,*
> *Tsunkawiye, Tsunkawiye*
> *Sauh! Sauh! Sauh! Sauh!*

My uncle Red Bird taught me that song, which must be sung four times, imitating that snort of the deer—*Sauh!*—after each verse. No boy's uncle could have been a better teacher. He also taught me to rub my feet in the ashes of the fire before singing it and then setting out.

But no one has ever taught me a song that will keep away the memory of harsh and unkind words.

Perhaps Uncle Red Bird, my mother's smiling older brother, knew such a song, but if he did I will never hear him sing it. Almost a year has passed since he caught the coughing sickness and made the last walk

5

to the Night Land. I do not have the words to express how much I miss him. Remembering him just brings back the pain I felt when his spirit passed from us. I need to turn my thoughts elsewhere.

Sitting here on the steps of my mother's cabin, I can hear her moving around inside. She is making more noise than she usually does when she is cooking, banging the rough wooden spoon I carved for her against the iron pot. She is making squirrel stew.

That's no surprise to me. I am the one who sat patiently under the oak trees as Great Sun walked slowly up into the morning sky, casting her light down on me through the leafless branches. As always, I had taken six long blowgun darts with me and one short one. I had already fired that first short dart at random, sending it off into the woods as an offering and for good luck.

I held my long blowgun steady, pointing it up where I knew the squirrel would appear. Only my lips moved as I imitated its call, knowing its curiosity would be too much for it.

Soon I heard the scrabbling of the first squirrel's claws against the bark high above me. I drew in a deep breath and then—as soon as it leaned out from the trunk to peer down at me—*whooot*! My aim was

6

true and the first squirrel landed at my feet, its heart pierced by my dart.

"*Saloli*," I said, placing a little tobacco next to it as my uncle taught me to do. "*Wado*."

I picked up the leaves which had been marked by the squirrel's blood when it fell and placed them at the base of the tree where I could easily find them. When my hunting was done, I would make a fire and take all of those leaves and burn them. In that way I would both remove the traces of my hunting and make an offering of thanks to the ancient fire.

When a hunter remembers to do as I was taught by my uncle, then he will be successful. The game animals will take note of his proper behavior and agree to give themselves to him.

Then, with that first squirrel's warm body inside the game bag slung over my shoulder, I had moved on to the next tree where I knew I would find another squirrel.

As long as I always take care to say thanks in the proper way whenever I take an animal, I will not have to worry about *Awi Usdi*. *Awi Usdi* is the Little White Deer who is the guardian of all the game animals. Whenever he comes—as he always does—to sniff at any blood drops left behind, he can tell that I have

7

spoken the proper words, given thanks, and shown respect. He does not follow my trail to send me bad dreams and make my hands twisted with rheumatism so that I can no longer pull back a bow or hold a blow-gun steady as I did when I shot each of those four fat squirrels.

The scent of that squirrel stew drifts out to me. It smells so very good. My mother's cooking is the best in Willstown. And I am very hungry right now.

But even my hunger and the smell of my mother's cooking does not stop me from thinking about my father and the hard words being spoken about him. I cannot go anywhere around people without hearing such gossip. Ever since he has returned from the West, it seems as if his curious markings are all that anyone can talk about.

With the tip of my stick I scrape a rough drawing in the dirt at the foot of the steps. A body, a head with a big beak, two feet, and then wings. Most people would see that shape as a big bird. But would they recognize it as an eagle or would they think it a buzzard?

My drawing is not good. I scrape my stick across it to erase it from the ground.

Is there really a way to make shapes that are better

than just drawings of things. An animal, a bird, a plant. Can shapes be made that talk Tsalagi? Can our people really do as my father tells everyone he can now do? Or do writing and books really belong only to the language of the white men?

"Uwohali."

I turn at the sound of my name.

My mother is looking down at me from the doorway, an unhappy look on her face.

CHAPTER 2

MY MOTHER IS WORRIED

"Uwohali," my mother says, "what is troubling you?"

A little breeze comes up from the river and blows a loose strand of the dark hair in her braid across her round face.

"You know," I say.

"Ah." My mother sighs.

My mother is worried about my interest in my father.

Their marriage, my father's first marriage, ended years ago.

I was young then, but I remember that day very well.

"I can no longer live with you. You need to go." That is what she said to my father.

"Then I will leave," he said.

Their voices were calm as they had that conversation. Neither one of them seemed angry. It was just a decision that my mother made, and my father agreed to it. My father gathered his things together and moved out of her house, his tools clinking together in a soft rhythm in his bag as he walked away.

Of course, I stayed with my mother. That is our Tsalagi way. She did not worry about my growing up without a father. My uncle Red Bird lived right next to us and among our people it is a boy's uncle as much as his father who teaches him the things he needs to know. A Tsalagi boy always belongs to his mother's clan, not his father's. And my father had gone away before—for almost a year when he went to fight in the Red Stick War. He and the other Tsalagi soldiers won that war for the Americans and saved the life of General Andrew Jackson. It was when my father came back that my mother told him their marriage was over.

So his being away was nothing unusual to me. Back before he gave up liquor, when he was called "Drunken Sequoyah" by almost everyone, he had frequently gone off drinking with friends for days and days. So, even though I did miss hearing Sequoyah's gentle voice telling stories when he was home and sober, my mother was certain that having my uncle Red Bird more than made up for my missing father.

I suppose she was right. While Red Bird was alive, I hardly ever thought of my father. That was especially easy over the last six years during which he was in Arkansas. Sequoyah was one of the party of Cherokee settlers who left Tennessee a few years after the Red Stick War. They wanted to make a new life far from the white men trying to drive them out of what was left of our homelands.

My father also had another reason for going west. It was to be in a place where he could work on his strange ideas without interference from suspicious neighbors. While Sequoyah had lived here during his last stay in Willstown—with the new wife he married after he and my mother parted—his strange behavior had resulted in his little work-cabin being burned.

But now, with Red Bird gone and my father back for some reason from the distant western lands, my thoughts seem to turn to him as regularly as the sun coming up in the east.

Since his return, my mother has not said anything bad about him. Whenever I have asked about him, her words have been careful.

"Was my father good at what he did?" I asked.

My mother nodded. "He was a talented silversmith," she said. "He was the best blacksmith in our town. Once he stopped drinking, he worked hard at whatever he chose to do."

"Was he unkind when he drank?" I asked. I wanted to know why their marriage had ended when I asked that question.

But my mother simply shook her head. "No," she said. "He was always a kind person."

"Why did he give up smithing if he was so good at it?"

"Your father has always had many ideas. And whenever he had a new idea, he would put aside what he had been doing before. He has always been very determined."

My mother paused then and looked out the window, as if remembering something. "It is just," she added, "that some of his ideas have been more useful than others."

My father now lives at the house of that second wife. Sally Guess, whom he married six years ago, is her name. She comes from a family even more prominent than my mother's.

Their marriage did not end after she destroyed his

work. He did not get angry at her about the fire. But when he went to Arkansas Sally Guess and their little daughter, Ahyokah, did not go with him. She preferred to remain close to her family here in Willstown and maintain her farm. However, she and Sequoyah did not divorce. She and Ahyokah have even visited him in Arkansas, and I understand that my father is quite close to my half sister.

Their big cabin and their farm are far over on the other side of Willstown. That cabin shows that Sally Guess comes from a well-off family. It is so large and well-built that it makes my mother's cabin look poor in comparison. Every now and then I see Sally and Ahyokah, who is now six, nearly the same age I was when my father left my mother's house. Whenever I've seen her, Ahyokah has seemed like a bright little girl—her dark, serious eyes darting everywhere, taking everything in. She also has a quick laugh that sounds almost like a robin's chirping. I suppose that to some people she would seem likable. I think I would find it rather irritating to be around her.

Still, I have to admit that seeing her has almost made me wonder what it would be like to have a little sister such as her, to not be the only young person in my mother's home. But that is not what I want. I have no desire at all to get to know her. I have never spoken to either her or her mother. I do not think they know who I am.

"Uwohali," my mother says again. "What is it?"

She already knows the answer. I do not have to say it. I want to go to the big cabin of my father's second wife on the other side of Willstown. I want to see my father. I want to ask him to teach me things.

"Why don't you want to keep learning from your uncles?" she asks. "There is still much they can teach you."

Her words are true. Red Bird was closest to me, but he was not my only uncle. His older brothers, Blackbird and White Raven, have a lot they could teach me. They know much about the new world in which our people must live. Both of them have learned to speak English. They are as well known by their English names of John and Samuel as they are by their Indian names. Both are deeply involved in the politics of our nation. The first elections for our new Tsalagi legislature take place this fall. Everyone says that one of them will surely be chosen to go to New Echota as one of the four representatives from our district.

15

But, unlike Red Bird, they both have children of their own and they are as devoted to them as my father, Sequoyah, was neglectful of me. They do not have all that much time for me. They travel so much and are so busy that I seldom see them.

Also, the path my mother's two remaining brothers have chosen is not really the one I want to follow. Politics does not interest me. I do not enjoy trying to convince people to like me better than they like someone else. I want to know how to make things, useful things.

Nor do I want to continue taking classes in English from the missionary, even though he has said I am a quick learner. No one, he told me, has learned to write the alphabet faster than me. And when I speak the *Aniyonega* words I have learned, I do so perfectly—or so he said.

That missionary, Reverend Worcester, is a kind man. Like many of the *Aniyonega* he likes our Tsalagi people and wishes to assist us. He believes that teaching us to read and write English will not just make it easier for him to "save our souls," as he puts it. He believes it will help us to resist being forced to leave our homeland.

I like Reverend Worcester. I like many of the other white people I have met. It is only some of the *Aniyonega*—those who are greedy for our land—who wish to drive us away. Unfortunately, those few who wish to get rid of us are powerful men. And one of the most powerful of those who wish to remove us is one who said he was our friend.

Perhaps that is why learning more English, which is the language of those who have betrayed and cheated us, does not interest me.

"Uwohali," my mother says, "did you hear what I just asked you?"

Ah, as it sometimes happens with me, my thoughts have made me drift away. What was it my mother asked? Oh yes, now I remember. She asked why I was so determined to go to see my father.

"My father can teach me how to work silver," I say. "He can teach me to work iron at his forge. Everyone says that no one can draw or paint, or carve, or do blacksmithing as well as my father."

My mother nods.

"That is true," she agrees. "Sequoyah is a great artist. When we were first married he drew a picture of a redbird for me. It was so real I thought that it would spread its wings and fly up off the page. And as I have told you before, no one was a better blacksmith."

Then she takes in a deep breath, as she always does

when she has not yet made her point. "He could teach you. But will he? Does he do any of that these days? All he does is show people his strange markings and tell them stories that are . . ."

My mother pauses. She wipes her hands down her apron as if dusting off flour. I know what word she was about to say before she stopped herself. It is the word everyone uses to describe my father. Crazy.

I don't reply. I stand up and take a few steps forward to look out at the river. This is a conversation we've had before. Seven times by my count—at least once every few days since Sequoyah's return.

I hear my mother sigh again from behind me. Then I hear her feet coming down the steps and walking toward me. I turn to look at her.

She pushes that strand of long hair back from her face. She puts her left hand on my shoulder. She has to reach up to do that. Though I am only thirteen, I'm taller than she is.

"Uwohali," she says, "my big eagle."

My mother's hands are strong from all the work she does. Chopping and carrying wood, repairing the fences that hold in Complainer, our mule, feeding the pigs, and milking the three cows. She even takes a hand in the plowing, which we will soon be doing when the days have grown a little longer and all the frost is out of the earth. Everyone says that she is stronger than most men. My uncles and I are always ready to help, but just as often as not she shoos us off and says that she wants to do it herself.

So when she squeezes my shoulder it hurts a little. But not quite as much as the pain I begin to feel in my heart. For I can sense that she is finally about to grant me permission to do what I want.

"You need to go," she says to me. Then she takes her hand from my shoulder and walks back into the cabin.

You need to go.

Those are the same words she spoke years ago to my father.

Those words ended their marriage. No Cherokee man would be foolish enough to try to argue when a Cherokee woman tells him that their marriage has ended. When women speak, men must always listen.

But I know that her words to me, though the same, hold a different meaning. My father will never again be her husband. But I will always be her son.

My mother says I am as stubborn as my father. She says I am like him in the way that I will not give up once my mind is set on something.

I just hope that I will succeed.

"Uwohali."

My mother is standing at the door of the cabin with a bowl of squirrel stew in her left hand and a big piece of corn bread in her right. There is a smile on her face again.

"Your squirrels will be upset if you do not eat the stew they gave you before you leave," she says.

CHAPTER 3

SITTING AND THINKING

I am sitting with my back against an oak tree, passing my chunkey stick back and forth from one hand to the other. It did not take me long to walk here. But I have been here for some time now, long enough for the sun to climb beyond the middle of the sky. People I know have walked or ridden by me. Some have nodded or raised a hand in greeting.

"*Osiyo*, Uwohali."

"*Osiyo.*"

But they have seen from my posture that I do not wish to be disturbed. Our people are very good at reading such subtle signs. If you do not wish to be bothered, they will leave you alone.

But that does not keep them from gossiping about you. What was cooked in a very small pot but provided more that enough for everyone to eat? The answer to that riddle is gossip. Although there are many people here in Willstown, it seems as if everyone always knows what everyone else is doing—or is said to have done. That is especially true if you are the son of the man more people are talking about now than any other person.

"I saw the son of Sequoyah. He was sitting in the cold under a tree and staring at the house where his father is staying."

"Ah, that is sad."

"*Uu*! Yes. I think that poor foolish boy hopes his crazy father may be able to teach him something."

But they may end up saying worse things than that. From the gossip I've heard, some people are deeply suspicious of him. Some are even saying that Sequoyah is an evil sorcerer. He went west only to learn more magic and has returned to work bad medicine on people. One of those is the man who just rode past me with a sour look on his face. He saw me but did not even nod his head in my direction. His name is Tall Man and he is the father of my friend Galuloi.

I am sure that when Tall Man gets home he will tell everyone in his family where he saw me. He may even tell his son to keep away from me.

My stepmother's place is impressive. It is not just the sturdy well-built log cabin that is bigger than my mother's. Though the two chairs on the porch are empty, smoke is rising from the chimney, and I know that someone is home. The place is well kept. It does not look as it did just before my father went to Arkansas.

I was heeding my mother's words back then and staying away from my father. So I did not see how it appeared when he was living there. But I am told that everything was looking run-down. Tall grass and weeds grew in the garden behind the cabin. When he left and my stepmother began taking care of things herself everything improved.

Of course appearance is not the most important thing. In fact, if you are too proud of how good your property looks or how handsome or beautiful you are, people may remind you of the story about Possum and his tail.

Back long ago, Possum was very proud of how he looked. The hair on his tail was thick and bushy, long and silky. He was always combing it and boasting about how beautiful it looked. He would sing this song about that tail of his:

He nio dil dil
Ha que que la lo

The other animals got tired of hearing him boasting like that. They got tired of hearing him always singing that irritating song again and again.

He nio dil dil
Ha que que la lo

So they went to Cricket.

"Go to his house at night," they said to Cricket. "Cut all the hairs off his tail while he is sleeping."

So Cricket did as they asked. He waited till Possum was asleep and then crossed over the creek to Possum's house. He cut off all the hairs on Possum's tail and then crept away.

The next day, Possum woke up and started to comb his tail as he always did every morning. But when he did so, all of those hairs came right off because Cricket had cut them.

And ever since then Possum has had the ugliest tail of all the animals.

Even though I was very young then, I remember my father's soft voice telling that story. It was not long after he told it that he left us when my mother ended their marriage.

I wish I had heard more of his stories, stories that I am sure he has told the daughter he had with my stepmother, Sally Guess. The thought of him telling her stories instead of me makes me feel sad—and also jealous of this half sister I've only seen but never met.

Next to the house is my stepmother's store. Sally Guess has run it by herself for several years. Until he lost interest in it, my father worked there with her. Sequoyah was known by everyone as a friendly trader who would trust people and give them credit. He kept track of everything in a book. Because he never wished to learn to write English, he drew a sketch of each customer and then made little marks—circles and lines of different sizes—to indicate how much they owed him.

Storekeeping was something he had learned from his mother when he was a boy in Taskigee. Taskigee was one of our biggest and most important upper towns, located north and east of here on the Little Tennessee River. This was before the white men came and burned Taskigee, before our people were forced to give up our upper towns and move here. It was at Taskigee that my grandmother had met the white man named Guess who is said to have been my grandfather. I have heard that it was a brief romance, and he moved on without knowing that she would give birth to his son nine months later. I know little about him except that some say he was a soldier and others that he was a traveling trader. All he left behind him was the white name that my father has always used. George Guess.

I never met my grandmother, Wuhteh. She left this life and went to the Darkening Land before I was born. But I feel as if I know her from what my mother shared with me about her.

My mother told me about my grandmother six years ago, not long after my father left us. We were outside, sitting next to the fire, and she was making stew from the squirrels I'd shot with my blowgun. Even then, at the age of eight, I was putting Uncle Red Bird's lessons about hunting into practice.

"Wuhteh, your father's mother," my mother said as she stirred the pot, "she was a true Tsalagi woman, strong and independent."

I remember smiling when my mother said that because she might as well have been describing herself.

Even as a small child, I knew how strong my mother was.

"Left on her own," my mother continued, "without a husband and with a small child, your grandmother did not give up. After all, among our people a woman is always the head of the family. Clan members are just as important to her as any husband. And that is true for her children, who inherit that clan from their mother's side. That is why, like me, you belong to the Bird Clan while your father is Paint Clan just like his mother."

She held out a spoonful of the stew. "Here, taste this."

I remember how good that stew tasted. It was wonderful, as always. But before I could say anything my mother shook her head. "Needs more seasoning, doesn't it?"

My mother reached into one of her jars of herbs, crumbled up several dried leaves, and shook them into the pot.

"So," she said, "Wuhteh was not really on her own. With the help of her family and her other clan members, she began to trade. And she did well in that business, so well that when he was still a young boy, just a bit older than you, your father began to help her."

My mother paused and lifted her head toward the

sunset direction—as if someone was approaching. I looked, but there was no one to be seen. She shook her head and continued her story.

"It was not easy for your father. A childhood accident and sickness had weakened one of his legs and made him lame. But he made up for that by being a hard worker and he excelled at everything he tried. He took over the trading from his mother and did even better than she had done. He was also a great artist. He spoke well and was a wonderful singer. He had such a strong gentle voice. From the first day we met, I knew I wanted him for my husband."

My mother went back to stirring the stew. It seemed that she had finished her story, but I wanted to know more.

"Can you tell me?" I asked. "What was it like then with my father?"

My mother pushed back her graying braid and sighed deeply. "It was not easy," she said. Then she struck her stirring spoon hard against the side of the metal pot. "And now I will talk no longer because this stew is done."

I haven't thought of that conversation with my mother for a while. But now that Sequoyah has returned from Arkansas, all of those memories are coming back to me. And thinking about him makes me wonder again about what it was like in those days when my father was a young trader.

Back then our nation's boundaries were double what they are today and the peace town of Echota was the capital of our nation. Thousands of deer hides were brought in every year to my father's store in Taskigee by our Tsalagi hunters. Then the white men moved in and killed all of the deer. And then our leaders were forced to sign yet another treaty and Taskigee and Echota were lost to us.

We are like the man in a story that my father told me when I was little. I was too young to understand it then as I do now. Perhaps my father understood that, but also understood me well enough to know that I would not forget it and that its meaning would one day be as clear to me as it is today. Or maybe he just told me that story because he was feeling sad and had been drinking. The smell of alcohol was strong on his breath and his voice was slurred as he told the story.

"A Tsalagi man was sitting by the river on a log," my father said. "Along came a white man.

"'Can I join you, my friend?' the white man asked.

"'Yes, my friend,' the Tsalagi man answered.

moving over to make room for his new companion.

"But then another white man came along and another . . . and another.

"Each time the Tsalagi man moved over to make room. So it went until finally the Tsalagi man was pushed off the end of the log, fell into the river, and was swept away."

I remember how I waited to hear what happened next. Did the Tsalagi man drown? Were the white men ever punished for what they did?

But my father just shook his head, got up, and walked away, his steps unsteady from drink.

I need to stop thinking about such things. Those thoughts are darker than the feathers of a raven. I turn my gaze again to the buildings across the road from me.

Next to the house is a low-roofed open-sided building. It looks a little like an arbor, such as the one behind my mother's small cabin. Almost every Tsalagi home has such an arbor for the warm months of long days. That is when everyone moves outside to cook our food and sleep at night cooled by the breeze that comes up from the river.

But this building, a building that his second wife had made for my father's use, is not an arbor. The things that I can see within it are not meant for cooking. There's a forge, an anvil, and hammers. Though little used, it contains everything needed for the profession I would like to learn. It's a blacksmith shop.

My father, Sequoyah, was one of the first Cherokees to become a blacksmith. No one taught him that trade. He learned it the way we have always learned things—by watching. He went to the blacksmith shops of white men and sat outside, carefully observing them at their work. He saw how they used the bellows to make the fire hot enough to melt iron. He saw how their forges were constructed, how they used buckets of water to cool the red-hot metal. Then, when he knew enough, he began to do his own blacksmithing. Soon everyone was coming to him to get their horses shod or to have things made of iron.

Even before my father became a blacksmith, he knew a great deal about working with metals. When he was a young man he began melting down silver coins to make the sort of jewelry that is still much in demand among our people. I cannot count how many times I have seen Tsalagi men and women wearing silver nose rings or earrings or armlets or bracelets that bear the stamp GEORGE GUESS on them.

Those words of his name were the only words in English he knew. His friend, Charles Hicks, the son of a Tsalagi woman and a Scots trader, had been educated by the missionaries. Charles Hicks was the one who showed my father how to make the shapes that spelled out his English name. It was a smart way to advertise. Anyone who saw one of those beautiful objects made of silver would read his name and know who made it. They would know where to go if they wished to buy something like it. If my father had just kept at his silversmithing he might have been the most prosperous man in Willstown—had it not been for whiskey.

Because my father often did blacksmith work for white men, he had easy access to hard drink. He shared that whiskey with Tsalagi friends who liked strong drink as much as he did. They all were amused by the stories he would tell and the songs he would sing while he was drinking. But he was often too drunk to work.

I remember those days when I was little. I remember the smell of the whiskey everywhere in our cabin. That same smell hung heavy on my father's breath as I sat on his lap while he told stories.

32

I also remember the men who drank with him, some of whom were not as gentle as my father when the whiskey was thicker in their veins than their Tsalagi blood.

"Stay away from those men," my mother told me. And I did as she said.

Some nights when the men were drinking, my mother and I would not even sleep in our own house, but would take our blankets outside and sleep under the arbor out back. Some nights even, we would wake with snow on our blankets and frost in our hair.

Whiskey is a powerful thing. It is a spirit as strong as any of the monsters in our stories. I still am amazed that my father was able to finally escape it. Perhaps it troubled him when he saw the awful things others did when in the grip of the whiskey spirit. They would use all their money to buy whiskey. They would fight with their families and their best friends. Sometimes they would stab or shoot each other.

So, one day, he stopped drinking.

"I will never drink again," he vowed to my mother.

At first she did not believe him, but he kept his word.

From then on, Sequoyah never again drank. That was true even when he went off to war with the Cherokee Regiment. There was strong drink everywhere in the camp of Sharp Knife, as we Cherokees called General Andrew Jackson. Many Cherokee men who were part of that brief and bloody war drank to forget what they saw. But even then my father never touched whiskey.

At first my mother was happy because the drinking had stopped. But her happiness did not last long. Because after my father, Sequoyah, stopped drinking he moved on to something else. It was something that consumed him even more than whiskey did. It was his new passion for making strange markings. It stopped him from working silver or iron or doing anything useful for anyone. That, and not drinking, was why my mother ended their marriage.

The sun has moved herself another hand's width across the sky. And I have done nothing other than remember old stories and think about things that trouble me.

No one has visited the store. Is it because they know my father is here and they are afraid of the bad medicine he may be working with his markings? No one has come out of the cabin. The blacksmith shop has remained deserted.

Perhaps no one is home, even though smoke is still

rising from the chimney, and I am just wasting my time.

I am not accomplishing anything by sitting. I need to do something.

I stand up, dust myself off, and walk across the road. My whole body is tense. My mouth is dry and my heart is pounding. But I can't stop now. I force my feet to move until I am at the base of the wooden steps.

I lean my chunkey stick against the porch. Then I climb the steps, lift my hand, and place it on the door.

"Osiyo?" I call inside. "Hello? Is anyone home?"

◇❄◇ CHAPTER 4 ◇❄◇

I GREET YOU, YOUNG MAN

"I am coming," says a voice in Tsalagi.

The words are spoken so well, in a voice so gentle and friendly, that they almost sound like the start of a song.

I hear the sound of shuffling steps coming across the floor inside. Then the door swings open and a man is standing there before me. And though it is long years since I have seen him, I know him for my father.

He is smaller than I had expected. His face is older, too. Though his eyes, which sparkle as if lit from within by sunlight, are youthful. He is not clothed like a white man—as so many of our people now dress. His garments connect him back to the older ways of our people.

His head is wrapped in a red-and-white cloth. Another cloth is knotted around his neck and tucked into a white calico tunic. Over it all is a knee-length blue robe. There's a beaded belt around his waist. Instead of buttoned-up pants, like those I have on, he's wearing buckskin leggings. Soft deerskin moccasins, not stiff shoes, are on his feet. A long-stemmed pipe is in his left hand.

In a single glance I take all this in—as well as the look on his face. It's warm and welcoming. Has he recognized me as his son?

"*Osiyo,*" he says in that musical voice. "I greet you, young man."

"*Osiyo,*" I say. Then my voice sticks in my throat and I cannot say anything more. I've realized from his greeting that he has no idea who I am. His kind smile is simply the face that I have heard he shows to everyone, even those who speak badly of him.

"Who is it?" calls a woman's voice from farther back in the cabin. It has to be the voice of my stepmother, Sally Guess.

The sound of more feet crossing the cabin floor. Feet moving with quick certainty. Then a woman appears, pushing my father aside. She does not do so roughly. She is merely taking his place because it is her right. It is proper for a Tsalagi woman to stand in the doorway before her husband, to be the first to welcome a stranger. A gray cat comes pattering out to meow and

37

rub itself around her legs and then mine as we stand there.

I look at her. I've seen her before, but always from a distance. Taller than my father she's a good-looking woman. In fact, to my surprise, I can see that she bears some resemblance to my mother. She's much younger, though her hair is already streaked with gray. (Does every woman who marries my father, I wonder, get gray hair early?)

Sally Guess looks straight up into my eyes. Her nose is a bit sharper than my mother's. The look on her face is not hostile, but it is much less patient than his welcoming smile.

Who is this? What does he want?

"*Osiyo,*" I say. "It's me." This is all I can get out.

Both of them now stare quizzically at me. I can imagine the thought crossing their minds.

Is this skinny boy standing before us touched in his head?

I have to say something more. I bite my lip. I'm so confused that for a moment I forget my own name. I swallow, take a breath.

"Uwohali," I blurt out. "Uwohali," I say looking at my feet, but addressing my words to Sally Guess. "I am the son of your husband."

I risk a quick glance up at my father, then back down at my feet. "Your son," I say.

A hand reaches out and clasps my shoulder.

"*Atsuta*, my son," my father says. "It is you. You are welcome."

I look up, holding my breath, uncertain of what I may see in Sally's face. But her look of uncertainty is gone. In its place is something like a smile as she looks over at my father and then at me and then at my father again.

"Hmmm," she says, as if to herself. "I see how alike you are."

Then she gestures toward me. "Uwohali, son of Sequoyah. You are welcome into my home."

My father removes his hand from my shoulder. "Yes," he says. "Come in. There is food."

I step over the threshold. I can smell corn bread and some sort of stew. I realize that even though I ate this morning, I am already hungry again. Lately I have been so hungry that my mother has said she needs to take the bowl out of my hands when I have emptied it for fear that I will start chewing on it.

She has even joked that my appetite is more that of a hummingbird than an eagle. Eagles only eat once or twice a day, but a hummingbird never stops buzzing from flower to flower and catching insects.

Long ago, they say, Eagle and Hummingbird were invited to a feast. Eagle took a long time getting ready, making sure that his feathers were preened properly. He was the chief of the birds and wanted to look his best. But when he arrived at the feast, he found that Hummingbird had gotten there ahead of him. And Hummingbird had eaten all of the food.

Someone is tapping my elbow.

I look down. A little girl stands there. Her dark eyes shine as she looks up at me. I have never seen her close up before, but I know right away who it is. Ahyo-kah, my half sister.

It's not polite to stare. But I can't stop myself from staring at her eyes. They look so familiar to me. Then, with a sick feeling in my stomach, I realize why and I look away. Her eyes. They are the same as my father's. Not only has she been able to have my father all to herself, she even has his eyes. The same kindness and intelligence that I just saw shining out of the eyes of Sequoyah are also there in the eyes of my little half sister, Ahyokah. It troubles me to see that. It's not right!

"What's your name?" she asks.

"Uwohali."

40

My voice comes out as a growl, but she pays no attention to that. Instead, she smiles.

"Uwohali! Good." She places her hands on her chest. "I am Ahyokah. You are my big brother. It makes me happy to see you. After you eat you can meet my dolls. I know they want to be your friend."

Then she opens her arms and hugs me around my waist. That is as high up as she can reach since she is only six years old and I am tall for my age.

I'm not sure what to do. I feel uncomfortable. I don't want to like this little girl who took my place in my father's life. I want to say that I am not happy to see her. I don't want to meet her dolls. I don't want to be their friend or hers. But I don't say anything. I just stand there while she keeps hugging me and smiling.

My father clears his throat and we turn to look at him. There's a smile on his face that looks just like the one Ahyokah beamed up at me.

"Your brother is tall," he says, "but he is not a tree for you to climb, daughter. Come, the food is ready."

"Yes," Sally Guess says. "Sit here, Uwohali."

She pulls back a chair for me from the table. As I sit I take note of the fact that the table's legs are beautifully carved to look just like the legs of a deer. It has to have been crafted by my father.

In front of me on the tabletop is a pile of papers covered with markings. Sally picks them up. She lifts one eyebrow toward my father and motions as if she is going to throw them into the nearby fireplace. My father just chuckles and continues limping toward his seat at the head of the table.

Sally smiles and nods. Then she continues past the blazing fire to place those papers on a shelf near the door. I hadn't noticed it before. There are other papers there, some of them folded together like the letters I have seen at the missionary's place. There's also a book there. I can read its cover from where I sit. It is an English spelling book.

I'm confused. Why does my father have an English spelling book? It has always been said that Sequoyah cannot read English and he never speaks it. And why did Sally pretend she was going to throw my father's papers into the fireplace? And why was his chuckle when she did that answered by her smile. Then I remember the story of what happened just before my father left for Arkansas. It is a story that people have begun whispering about since his return. I've heard bits and pieces of it here and there—at the store, at the Council House, or on the ball field—being told by people who've stopped talking as soon as they've noticed me listening and recognized me as the son of the man about whom they were gossiping.

Gradually, though, I've been able to put those whispered scraps of story together—the way my mother sews patches of cloth together to make a quilt. And the pattern they've made, the tale they've shaped, is a troubling one. Here is the blanket of story I pieced together.

Sequoyah had stopped working at his forge. He no longer even helped Sally with the crops or the livestock. He had built a little cabin in the woods and spent all of his time there making marks on paper. When he ran out of paper he would take chips of wood and make marks on them.

The way he was acting made Sally worried, but what people said worried her even more.

"Your husband," a hunter who came to her cabin told her, "I think he is crazy. I found him sitting in the middle of the forest. He was playing with pieces of wood like a little child. He was talking to them. When I spoke to him, he did not reply. He did not even notice I was there."

Many people said that he had lost his mind. Others wondered if he was engaging in witchcraft. Was he making evil spells to hurt people? The old penalty for being a witch was death. Some began to whisper that perhaps Sequoyah should be killed before he brought harm to others. That worried Sally Guess and those who cared about him.

My father's best friend at the time was Turtle Fields. "Sequoyah," Turtle said. "People are worried about the strange way you are behaving. They say you are making a fool of yourself. You are going to lose your good name."

But my father just shook his head. "My friend Turtle, what I am doing is not foolish. What I am doing is for the people. And I shall go on doing it."

The whispers about my father grew stronger. It was said that one group of men was planning to waylay Sequoyah with rifles and shoot him to death.

Finally, those who cared about Sequoyah decided that there was only one way to turn my father from his dangerous path. They made a plan to hide themselves in the woods near his cabin while Sally drew my father away.

"My husband," Sally told him, "come with me. There is something you must see."

When Sequoyah was far enough away, his concerned neighbors came out of the woods and went into the little building. They were shocked at what they saw. Those symbols that might be witchcraft were not just drawn on pieces of paper and chips of wood. They were scrawled on the walls, carved into the table and the chairs. Those brave enough to go into that cabin only stayed long enough in that frightening place to set it ablaze. Because it was filled with all those papers and dry chips of wood, it took almost no time at all before the roof collapsed as the flames roared up.

My father came back to the cabin almost as soon as it started to burn. Perhaps he had smelled the fire or seen the smoke rising. But he did not behave as Sally and the others had expected. He didn't try to put out the fire or save anything. That's what I would have done if everything I'd worked hard to make was destroyed. I might also have shouted in anger or wept in despair. But not my father. He just stood by, his face calm as he watched it burn. That was strange.

But even stranger is what they say he did when it had all burned to ashes. He stuck one finger into them and rubbed it on his palm, leaving a black streak. Then he stood up and . . . smiled.

"Hawa," he said, "all right. Now I can have a fresh start."

45

Now, even though she helped destroy my father's work back then, my stepmother no longer seems worried about his markings. She can pick them up and move them. She can even joke about them.

Has she gone crazy, too? Should I leave this house before I am also made insane?

My father is saying something.

"*Wado*, *Edoda*. Thank you, Our Heavenly Father."

In his warm, gentle voice, he is thanking the Creator for the gift of this food we are about to eat. It calms me, takes away some of my uncertainty.

A big bowl of stew is put in front of me along with a slab of corn bread even larger than the piece I ate this morning in my mother's cabin. Next to it, Ahyokah places a cup filled with cider, smiling up at me as she does so.

"*Wado*," I say, before I think. "Thank you."

That makes Ahyokah's happy smile even broader. It's hard for me not to smile back at her, but I keep my face expressionless. I do not want her to think I like her or that I am going to treat her like a big brother. I do not have time for that. I did not come here to make friends with this little girl, but to meet my father.

I turn my attention back to the food. Everything

looks and smells so good that my mouth is watering.

"Eat," Sally says. "Put some meat on those long limbs of yours."

"Eat," my father says.

"Yes," my little sister says in that irritatingly sweet voice of hers. "Eat."

I eat.

CHAPTER 5

AHYOKAH'S FRIENDS

My father sits quietly, leaning back in his chair and not watching me as I eat.

I am glad of that. It is not just because it is always best to eat and then talk. You should always show respect for your food by giving it your full attention. It is also that it gives me some time to collect myself. I am uncertain and excited at the same time. Even though it has been a long time since I have seen my father, even though he left me, I am not feeling resentment toward him right now. Instead, I find myself liking him. His voice and his face are both so kind. I cannot understand how anyone could imagine him wanting to do anything to hurt another person.

I look over at him and he nods his head, a little smile twisting his lips as he does so.

Eat, he is telling me.

I eat.

I finish one bowl of stew. It has onions and turnips and chunks of beef, all floating in a thick brown broth. Of course it is not as fine as my mother's cooking, but it is good.

"More, Uwohali?" my stepmother says, bringing the pot over to me.

"Wado!" I reply as I accept another bowlful and then hold up my empty cup so that my sister can fill it again with cider.

When I am done, Ahyokah tugs at my sleeve.

Leave me alone, I think.

But she tugs at my sleeve a second time.

I turn to look at her, even though I wish she would just leave me alone. I don't want to spend time with her. I haven't come here to get to know her but to learn something useful from my father.

"Are you ready to meet my dolls?" she asks.

I want to say no.

Not now, I think. But before I can reply she turns toward Sequoyah.

"Father, can I show Uwohali my friends now?" she asks.

A warm smile creases my father's face. It's clear that

49

he will agree to anything my half sister asks of him.

I feel a surge of anger toward this little girl who took my place. But I don't let that emotion show on my face, even though my hands squeeze the wooden table-top so hard that my knuckles turn white.

"Uh-huh," Sequoyah says. "If it is agreeable with your brother."

He looks at me. What can I do? I nod my reluctant head.

"Good," my father says. He holds up his long-stemmed pipe. "I will be on the porch."

Ahyokah takes my hand and leads me to the back of the cabin. Her three corn-husk dolls, made in the proper way with no faces, are sitting there on a minia-ture bed that I am certain was carved by my father. It makes me feel even more jealous of all the attention he has given her, attention I never received.

Yet, at the same time, I can't stop myself from ad-miring the workmanship that went into making that little bed and my sister's little friends. I sit down cross-legged on the floor to look closer at them. They are not at all like the dolls that non-Tsalagi children have, like the one I saw once being held in the arms of a white child who was being driven by in a carriage. That white child's doll had such a shiny, humanlike face that I found it disturbing to see.

Ahyokah's three friends were made in our old way from dried corn husks folded and tied together to make a head, a body, and two arms. Each one is dressed like a Tsalagi woman. And, of course, they do not have faces on them.

My little sister is leaning her head against my shoulder.

"Do you know why corn-husk dolls never have a face?" I ask.

"Can you tell me why?" she asks.

And almost before I know it I am telling her the story.

"It was because of the first of their kind. Long, long ago, that first corn-husk doll was so good-looking that everyone admired her. Everyone talked about how beautiful she was. Corn-Husk Doll heard what people said and she became vain.

"'No one is as beautiful as I am,' she boasted.

"She began to spend much of her time looking at her reflection in the water and admiring herself.

"'I am so beautiful,' she would say. 'I am so very beautiful!'

"One day, though, as Corn-Husk Doll sat gazing at her face in the water, those waters were rippled by the wind. And then, just like that, her face disappeared from her head. Ever since then, no corn-husk doll has had a face. And so we tell all our little girls that story to remind them to not be vain and boast about their good looks."

Ahyokah climbs into my lap and gives me a hug.

"That was such a good story," she says. "You are just as good as Father at telling stories."

Despite my desire to have nothing to do with this little sister I've just met, it seems that all I have done is make her like me more. Plus I am finding it harder to dislike her. I can't help but feel some pride about what she said—that I am like my father in some way. It actually feels pleasant to have her sitting in my lap like this with her head leaning back against my chest. I'm not sure I like the way it is making me feel protective of her. I cannot think of what to do or say. I look over at the three corn-husk dolls.

I carefully disentangle myself from her arms.

"Can you tell me about your friends?"

"Oh yes!" Ahyokah says, hopping out of my lap like a little squirrel leaping down from a stone. She gathers up the three dolls and brings them back to me.

"They are my best friends, and they are always happy to see me. And that is good because the other girls of my age do not want to play with me."

For a moment, a sad look starts to come over her happy face—like a cloud moving in front of the sun. I suddenly realize that whatever suspicion people might have about me visiting my father, it must be much worse for Ahyokah, who is living in the same house with him. But that sad look passes quickly and her eager smile comes right back again.

"They are sisters, you know. That is why they all look alike. This one is Meli," Ahyokah says, handing me the first doll. "She is pleased to see you."

"*Osiyo*, Meli."

"And this is Madi and this is Losi."

"*Osiyo, osiyo,*" I say.

Ahyokah looks pleased.

"How do you know who is who?" I ask.

"It is easy," Ahyokah says. "Meli has the blue sash, Madi has the red sash, and Losi has the white sash."

Ahyokah is so serious that I cannot resist teasing her. "But what if their sashes fell off? How could you tell which one was which? After all, you said they are sisters and all look alike."

Ahyokah giggles. "Silly," she says, "I can always tell them apart."

She takes the doll she called Losi from my hand and turns her around.

"See!"

On the back of the doll are two shapes carefully marked in ink. They look familiar to me because I have seen them before in one of the missionary's books he called a primer. He uses that book to teach us the twenty-six letters in the English alphabet, letters that I have already learned. One resembles a capital **G**. The other looks like a small **b**.

"Ah," I say. Then I speak the letters. "Gee bee."

Ahyokah looks up at me. "What is geebee?"

I point at the two inked shapes. "Gee and bee," I say.

"Tlahhuh!" Ahyokah says. "No!" She puts her little finger on the two shapes one after the other. *"Lo,"* she says. *"Si."*

I'm confused, confusion that grows strong when she takes her other two dolls and shows me the marks on their backs.

"Meli," she says. "**ᎾᎵ** *Me*" and "**Ꮧ** *li*."

"Madi," she says. "**ᎠᏍ** *Ma*" and "**Ꮧ** *di*."

Those marks look nothing at all like any of the twenty-six letters I have learned from the missionary.

"Ahyokah," someone calls from behind us. It takes a moment for me to realize it is my stepmother.

"Yes, Mother?"

"Now that your brother has met your dolls, let him go out on the porch with your father. You can come help me clean up."

Ahyokah looks up at me again. I know what that look on her face means. I suspect it is on mine whenever my own mother calls me away from something I am doing. I grin at her and then look up toward the roof of the cabin.

What can we do except what our mothers ask us to do?

Ahyokah sighs, then gives me a little conspiratorial smile and nods.

What, indeed?

"I am coming, *Etsi*," she says.

And as soon as she dances out of the room it feels empty. Am I missing her presence? Despite my best efforts, have I begun to like this little half sister I was so determined to ignore?

CHAPTER 6

MARBLES

There are two chairs on the small porch of Sally Guess's house. My father has settled himself peacefully into one of them and has already lit his pipe. Every now and then he lifts it from his lips and lets a little cloud of smoke drift up from his lips.

I have seen how some old people smoke. They puff hard on their pipes and chew the stems. They make it seem more like work than something that relaxes them. But it seems that even smoking, like everything my father does, is something that he does with a sort of gentle ease.

He nods his head toward the other chair. I settle in next to him.

As we sit there, neither of us speaking, I begin to wish I had something to occupy my hands as he does with his pipe. Young people do not smoke. It is that way with our people, unlike the white men who seem to use tobacco all the time, whether they are young men or older. We *Anitsalagi* believe that tobacco is too special for that. It is something that the Creator gave as a gift. Young men may smoke the pipe with others in a ceremonial way as a sign of peace. But solitary smoking is meant only to ease the lives of those who are elderly. Although even the elderly should not smoke all the time because it might make them sick.

My father finishes the pipe, taps it out into his hand, and then gently blows away the ashes. *"Wado,"* he says to the little wind that swirls away the ashes.

Then, as he tucks the pipe in his vest pocket, he turns to me and says:

"Back when the world was new," he says, "there were seven old men who were leaders of their people. It was a time when there was fighting going on and it was the job of those old men to bring peace. But when they gathered together, they did not talk about peace. All they did was to bend their heads over their pipes and keep smoking, even though the proper time to do so would have been after peace was made. The smoke rose up from their pipes and turned into clouds.

"They smoked for seven days and nights. Seeing what those old men were doing, the Creator was not pleased. Instead of trying to bring peace, they were just smoking. So he turned those seven elders into those grayish-white flowers that bend over like old men smoking pipes.

"Today those pipe flowers, which are the color of an old person's hair, grow wherever friends and relatives have been quarreling to remind them to try to find peace."

My father looks off to the east, toward the big mountains that rise there.

"And the Creator also made smoke that stays over the mountaintops as a further reminder. It will remain there until the day comes when everyone finally learns to live in peace."

The story finished, my father settles back into that companionable silence of his. I feel comfortable sharing that silence. You do not always have to be talking to communicate with someone. And that silence gives me time to think about that story and about tobacco.

All of us *Anitsalagi* like to have tobacco with us

wherever we go. It is such a sacred plant, such a gift from the Creator. When we gather medicine or hunt, we offer tobacco as a sign of our gratitude. That way the balance is made right. You should never just take from the world without giving something back. I think back on the day when I gathered the clay for my marbles. I made a little indentation in the clay bank and put some tobacco there.

My marbles.

I have them with me in my pocket. All of my friends and I carry our marbles with us whenever we leave our homes. That way if we meet a friend or two along the way we can sit down together, scratch a circle into the earth, and have a game. And although I may not be as good a player as my best friend Yugi, I always come away with at least as many marbles as I started with.

I reach in my pocket and feel their comforting solid shapes with my fingertips. I pull several of them out and roll them around in the palm of my right hand, letting them click against one another.

All of the marbles I make are quite round. None of them have any cracks in them. But they do not look alike. They are different sizes and colors. The small ones are quicker to make. The clay doesn't have to be completely dry when you put them into the fire to harden them. And the various colors come from both the different clays that are used and the type of wood with which you make your fire. If you choose yellow locust, the same tree from whose saplings we make bows, you will get a fire that gets very hot very fast. If you use *tsiyu*, the tulip poplar from whose logs we make our houses and which was used in the past for our canoes, the fire will not be so hot and the color of the marble will be lighter.

Whenever you make marbles, you should not hurry. You should place the balls of clay that will become your marbles carefully so they are not touching one another. You should pile the split pieces of wood just right and make sure that the fire is burning evenly. Then you should wait until it has all cooled down before trying to take your marbles from the fire. Do not be impatient. Otherwise you may end up with burns on your hands from those still hot marbles, burns that may turn into scars—like the ones on the thumb and index finger of my impatient friend Ugama.

"You made all of those?"

I hadn't noticed, as I rolled those marbles about in my hand, that my father had leaned over to look at them.

"Uh-huh," I reply. Then my tongue sticks in my mouth. I am not sure what to say next.

My father reaches out one long finger to tap it against one of the marbles. It's a medium-sized brown marble with a slightly pitted surface.

"Not this one," he says.

He's right. That marble is one that I won in a game with Galuloi and Ugama. At the end the three of us came out even, but that brown marble was one Ugama made. The shortest and roundest of my friends, he is also the fastest runner. But, though his speed is certainly a gift, his lack of patience is not. Whenever he fires his marbles, he always does it in such haste that some always end up either breaking or being imperfect like this one.

But that does not upset him. "It doesn't matter if the marbles I make are not as good as yours, Uwohali," Ugama sometimes says, a big grin on his round face. "Sooner or later I will win all of your marbles from you."

I smile as I remember that remark of his. Especially because I know it will never prove to be true.

My father nods at that smile of mine. "You won it from a friend and you are thinking of him right now," he says.

I nod.

"It is good to have friends," he says.

He picks up one of the marbles from my hand, the one I like the best. It is a milky blue color and almost as smooth as glass.

"Well made," my father says. "Are you good at making things?"

This time my voice does not fail me. "I like to make things, but I am not that good. I would like to learn how to be better. I am interested in learning."

And that is why I am here. I want you to teach me painting and carving and how to work silver and how to be a blacksmith.

That is what I think. But I do not say it.

My father settles back into his chair. "Interested in learning," he says in a low voice. He seems to be saying that to himself rather than to me. He reaches his hand up to his chin and strokes it with two fingers. "Hmmm."

What he says next surprises me.

"How is your mother?"

"My mother?"

"I have heard that she is well."

"Yes, she is." My answer is quicker, sharper than I

intended. I did not come here to talk about my mother.

"Does she know that you have come here to see me?" He nods toward my chunkey stick still leaning against the porch near the bottom of the steps. "Or did you tell her you were going to go and play with your friends?"

"Yes," I say. "I mean no. I mean . . ." I pause, trying to get my words right. I usually do not have trouble saying what I mean, but I am just so unsure where this conversation is going that my thoughts are tripping over each other like clumsy runners in a race. I take a breath. "Yes, I told my mother that I was going to visit you."

"Even though she disapproved of it?" He asks that as a question to which he already knows the answer. And his tone is mild, his words followed by one of those warm chuckles that seem to be a natural part of his conversation.

"*Osdadu*," he says, "it's all right. Of course your mother would be worried about your wishing to see your crazy old father."

I start to say something, but he raises his hand.

"I know what everyone says, that my mind is not right. Just as I know that it was not easy for your mother when we were together. She had good reason for ending our marriage. Just as I had good reason for staying on this path." He looks out from the porch as if looking at something a long way away.

I follow his gaze, but all I can see is the road, the bare trees, the land beginning to slope down toward the river.

"But still your mother did not stop you." My father is nodding his head again. "She has always been wise, your mother. She knows that trying to keep your child from doing something seldom produces the result you wish."

He looks back at my carefully notched stick. "Do you know the story of the seven boys who were always playing chunkey?"

I think I do. I cannot remember a time when I didn't love to listen to stories. My uncle Red Bird used to say that my hunger for stories was almost as great as my hunger for food. Red Bird.

I cannot keep a sad look from coming to my face as I remember my uncle. I've been missing him so much.

"What is troubling you?" my father says in a soft voice. And then, almost as if he can read my mind, he leans closer. "Are you thinking of your uncle?"

I nod. "How did you know?"

"I heard of his passing," my father says, his voice

almost a whisper, meant for my ears alone. "Red Bird was my friend, you know. We grew up together. Although I could not be there with you, I knew that he would teach you well. No boy could have had a finer uncle."

I'm not sure what to say. My father's sympathy has touched me so deeply that I feel a lump in my throat. Then a little voice from inside the cabin speaks up.

"Would you tell that story about the seven boys, *Edoda*? Please, Father, please!"

CHAPTER 7

THE CHUNKEY PLAYERS

Of course it is Ahyokah. My father knew she was there listening just as well as I did. He, too, probably heard her open the door just a crack behind us soon after we sat down. That is why he lowered his voice to whisper those words about Red Bird to me. Though he is growing older, it seems as if his senses have not become dulled.

He looks over at me and shakes his head. "You see how it is around here," he says. "I can never say anything without your little sister hearing it. Even if there is nothing worth hearing from my old mouth."

Ahyokah pushes her way out through the door, walks straight over to our father, and plops herself down at his feet.

"That is NOT so!"

"Must I tell that story? Even if I cannot tell it well?"

"Yes, you must! You are a great storyteller, Father."

I am both pleased and irritated right now. I'm pleased that my father may be about to tell another story. But I am irritated that my little sister has thrust herself right into the middle of this special time I was having with him. She has him every day when he is at home. She also has been with him in the western lands. Over the last three years, from what everyone says, she and her mother have often traveled west to see him, spending weeks and weeks at a time in his company while Sally's two brothers took care of her farm and house. This is the first time I've been with my father in so long. It should be my time with him, not hers. Doesn't she understand that?

But of course she doesn't. She may be bright, but she is just a little girl. And because she seems to like everyone—including the grumpy big brother who just walked into her life—she probably can't even imagine how jealous I am feeling about her. She is such a likable child. If she were anyone else's daughter I would probably think she was adorable and not like a splinter stuck in my foot.

I shake my head. It has come to me that I should be

ashamed of myself. How can I be thinking in such a selfish way? Ahyokah is a big part of my father's life. And she does not seem to have any problem about sharing him with me. I am the one who has the problem. I am the one who is the problem.

I think of my uncle Red Bird. I can almost hear his calm voice reminding me that whenever I am feeling unhappy, I should ask myself who is causing that unhappiness. Is it someone else's fault or is it my own? Right now, I know the answer to that question. My jealousy is not Ahyokah's doing. It is mine. And even if she does have my father all the time, she also has no friends because of that, aside from her three dolls. That cannot be easy for her.

I need to turn my mind around and change my thinking. If I want to know Sequoyah—to learn from him—then I will have to accept my new sister as part of the bargain.

A small hand reaches up to take my hand. I look down at Ahyokah who has slid over to sit in front of me. She is nodding her head, her lips pressed together in a look of triumph.

"Father will tell us that story now," she whispers up to me.

"Long, long ago," his voice takes on that slow, sure rhythm I always associate with our oldest tales, "there were seven boys who were great friends. All of them loved playing chunkey. They would spend most of their days down by the town house in the middle of their village playing the game. One after another, each of them would roll a chunkey stone while the others would slide their sticks along the ground trying to knock it over. And if no one succeeded in striking it, they would measure whose stone came closest to the place where it stopped rolling, using the notches in their sticks.

"They loved their game so much that they did not go to the fields to guard the corn from birds and animals or do anything to help. They hardly ever came home except to eat, and their mothers grew impatient. They scolded those seven boys, but it did no good. Finally, the mothers got together and decided to do something. That night when those boys came home, their mothers served them a soup with no corn in it. The only things in the broth were chunkey stones that their mothers had gathered up and boiled. 'Because you like chunkey better than corn, this is what you must have for your dinner.'

69

"This made those boys very angry. 'It was wrong for our mothers to treat us this way,' they said. 'Let us do something.' They went down to the town house and began to dance around and around. Around and around they danced.

"Their mothers got worried when their sons did not come home. They went down to the town house to look for them. There they saw their sons angrily dancing around and around. But no dust was being kicked up by their feet—for as they danced they were rising up into the air. The mothers tried to reach their children and pull them back down, but they were already dancing up above the roof of the town house. One mother grabbed a long chunkey pole and managed to strike it against her boy, who was the last in line. It pulled him down, but he struck the ground so hard that he sank down out of sight into the earth.

"Those other six boys kept on dancing, rising higher and higher until they became stars. Those same six stars dance around the sky together to this day, reaching the top of the sky in the middle of winter every year. And where that seventh boy struck and sank into the earth, up grew that tall tree we now know as *osgutanuhi*, the pine."

Ahyokah looks up at me. "You see," she says. "I knew it would be a good story. My father is the best storyteller. Are you not glad I made him tell that story to us?"

"*Wado*, little sister," I say. "I am glad, indeed."

Ahyokah stands up, still holding my hand. "Now I know you want to spend some time by yourself with Father. So I will leave you two alone. Also, I should go back and help my mother. It is very hard for her to get all her work done without my help, you know."

My mouth has fallen open while Ahyokah is speaking. She understands so much more than I thought she did. Even though she is years younger, she is more mature than I am. I feel even more ashamed of myself for those jealous thoughts that I had to drive from my head. Rather than a rival, Ahyokah is an ally. No, more than that! This bright, friendly little girl whose gentle smile and voice are a perfect echo of my father's is my sister. My sister!

Now I am the one who wants to hug her.

Ahyokah presses her lips together in that way of hers that shows she knows she has gotten her way. Then she squeezes my hand one more time, turns, and vanishes back through the door as quickly as a squirrel scooting around a tree trunk.

My father laughs out loud.

"My son," he said, "you see who runs my life?"

There is such contentment in his voice that all I can do is nod—and enjoy the smile coming to my own face as I share his happiness.

"Now come with me," he says. He leans forward, resting his weight on his one good leg, and then rises from his chair in one easy motion. As always, despite his disability, there is such grace in everything my father does.

We go down the stairs together and walk the few paces across the yard that it takes to reach his unused smithy.

Is he going to teach me something about blacksmithing? I'm so excited that I find myself biting my lower lip.

He ducks his head to enter the low building, and I follow close behind.

"You know," Sequoyah says, picking up a hammer, "we are surrounded by the white men. Everywhere we look we see them and we think we have to copy them. We have to be like them to survive. Is that not what people say?"

"That is so," I agree.

"That is what I thought, also. So I learned the things

72

they know. I traded as they trade. I learned to work metal the way they do. And I made things that were of use. Like this." He turns the hammer so that I can see the handle. "And then I marked them this way."

I read the words carved in English into the hickory-wood handle.

GEORGE GUESS.

My father puts his finger on those words.

"Your name," I say.

"That is my name as the white men would have it," he replies. "I learned how to write that name from my friend Charles Hicks, the one who is now the head of Willstown."

He passes the hammer to me, and I heft it in my hands. It fits my palm perfectly, and it feels good. It is so solid and perfectly balanced a tool that it seems to be speaking to me, begging to be used, ready to be of service.

"I should put my name on each thing I make. That is what my friend Charles told me. Then everyone will know who the maker is. When they want something like that, they know who to ask to make it. And his words were wise. It happened just that way. Soon many people were coming to ask me to make hammers and other useful tools such as this."

He picks up a knife and hands it to me. I put down the hammer on top of an anvil and take the knife. It, too, is marked with his English name. It feels even better in my hand than the hammer did. This knife is so well made that it balances in my hand perfectly. I observe the way it has been sharpened, not as the white men do, but in our Tsalagi way. Rather than honing both edges on the cutting side of a knife, we only sharpen one.

I try to hand the knife back to him, but he doesn't notice. While I've been studying this knife, he has turned his gaze out of the shop. What is he looking at? His eyes seem again to be focused on the road outside—as if expecting to see something there. But all I see is a wagon passing by with a Tsalagi family in it. All of the people in that wagon—a man, a woman, and several children—are quiet and carefully averting their gazes from us. They are far away and their faces are turned from us so that I cannot recognize any of them, though that does look like one the wagons owned by my friend Ugama's uncle.

It appears as if those people are worried that looking our way might bring them bad luck or worse. The woman next to the man is hunched and even has her shawl over her head. There is nothing more terrifying to most Cherokees than witchcraft. We are even more frightened of that than we are of the white men.

As if to prove the truth of what I thought, the man driving the wagon lifts his left hand in our direction. He makes a sign that is meant to keep black magic away. My father does not seem to even notice that. He is looking far beyond that passing wagon.

"I was glad to get the business. But the thought of having to use the language of the white men to identify the things I made troubled me," he said. "Why did we have to use their language? Why could we not use our own? Our language is as beautiful to hear as the singing of the birds. Why would we not want to keep hearing the birds sing?"

Language? I did not come here to talk about language.

Why is he telling me this? I am no longer sure what this is all about. The only thing I am becoming sure of is that he is not about to teach me anything regarding blacksmithing today.

"I need to go," I say. I try to hand the knife back to him, but he raises his hand, palm out.

"Wait."

He begins searching with both his hands along one of the shelves. When he turns back to me he is holding a knife sheath in each of his hands. The first is strung on a rawhide cord, the old style that would be worn around the neck. He looks at me, shakes his head to himself, and puts that sheath back in its place. Then he hands me the second one, the one with a loop on the back so that it can be hung from a belt like the one I wear around my waist.

"Here," he says. "I give you this sheath. You can use it to hold that knife. I loan you that knife. See what you can make with it."

I understand his words. To give someone a knife may mean that you wish to cut the ties between you. But to just borrow it, even if you never give that knife back, it keeps that connection.

"*Wado, Edoda,*" I say as I slip the knife into the sheath, noticing as I do so that my father has decorated the sheath with a series of designs.

I am feeling happy, moved by his gesture. But before I can slip the knife in its sheath onto my belt, Sequoyah does something strange.

He takes his pipe out of his vest pocket, wets the index finger of his right hand, and sticks it into the pipe bowl.

"ᏐᏩᏖᏗ," he says slowly, using the residue of ash on his finger to make marks on top of the bench next to him. "Knife."

I look at those four marks in spite of myself. The first looks like a *B*, the second resembles a *W*, but the other two are nothing at all like letters in the English alphabet. In fact, I realize with a start, they are the same designs on the underside of the sheath he just gave me.

My father smiles. "ᏌᏫᎣᏗ *Yelasidi*," he says again, his finger touching each of those shapes as he does so.

A strange thing is happening to me. I actually am feeling myself drawn to those marks. It is as if they really are alive, as if they are speaking to me, trying to tell me something. I feel excited by that. But then I begin to feel another way—fearful! Is my father putting a spell on me? It is said that when someone begins to work evil medicine, they may use certain signs to draw you in, to steal your spirit.

Is my father's kind smile and gentle voice just a disguise to hide that he has become one who works black magic? I've also heard it said that when someone wishes to become powerful in that bad way that they must sacrifice one of their own family members to gain such power.

Should I take that sheathed knife from my belt and throw it on the ground? Part of me wants to do that. But another part is telling me not to do anything rash.

It is telling me to trust my father, keep this knife that he has given me.

But what should I do now?

I stand there for a moment, as still as a figure carved from wood.

Then speaking my words slowly and with great care I say, "I have to go now," and walk out of Sequoyah's shop.

CHAPTER 8

CONFUSED THOUGHTS

This morning, when I wake up in my mother's house, I feel more confused than I have ever felt before. I am in the familiar room where I went to bed last night. I am in the same bed I have slept in since I left my mother's side and began to sleep on my own. Yet today everything around me seems strange.

What is it? The window is where it has always been. The logs that make up the walls have not moved or changed their shapes. There's the place by the window frame where I tried scratching my name, in the letters of the alphabet that the missionary taught me.

Uwohali Guess.

And there is my chair. And next to it my shoes are resting where I took them off last night. My shirt is hung over the back of the chair, right on top of my pants.

So what is not the same?

Then the answer comes to me. Nothing around me has changed. It is what is within me. I am the one who has become different. It is as if my mind has divided itself into two opposing sides that are having a tug-of-war with each other.

One half is trying as hard as it can to pull me away from the influence of my father. There is danger there, that side is chanting. He may be evil. Go back to him and you may be lost.

But the other side is pulling just as hard, if not harder. He has a voice that is gentle. His face shows no anger, no greed, no hatred. How can anyone who seems so kind be of harm to anyone—especially his own son?

And the image of those shapes he made on the bench, along with those on the backs of my sister's dolls come back to me.

ꞵ. The one like a *B*.

W. The one like a *W*.

And what were those two that Ahyokah read off the back of her doll. Like a big *G* and small letter *b*.

Ꮹ.

Ꮟ.

Then there are the designs on the underside of the knife sheath that rests now underneath my windowsill.

Ꮟ.

Ꮃ.

ᎣᎥ.

Ꮃ.

Why is it that I can remember them so well?

Aha. I shake my head to try to quiet both sides. I
need to think of something else.

"Atsuta?" my mother's musical voice calls from the
front of the cabin. "My son, are you awake? Are you
hungry?"

I smell the hominy and the bacon cooking. The
thought about the confusion in my mind fades. Nothing in the world can make me feel better than food,
especially the food my mother cooks.

"Uh-huh!" I call to her as I roll out of bed. "Yes!"

After I've eaten I feel even better. I spend some time
around the farm. It is good to keep busy. It is good to
keep your mind on the things you are doing and nothing else. I slop the hogs and feed the chickens. I fix
a door on our small barn that was starting to loosen
on its hinges. I bring in more wood for the fireplace.
I hum one of the Christian hymns that the missionary was teaching us when I went to his school. It has
a pleasant sound to it, that song about grace being an

81

amazing thing. I do not know all the words, but I have always been good at remembering tunes.

Ulelanugo, hmm hmm, hmm hmm

My mother sometimes says that I was born singing. I'm still humming that tune as I walk back to the cabin.

My mother is standing at the door. There is a look I cannot quite understand on her face.

"You are happy today, Uwohali," she says.

"That is true," I say.

She presses her lips together. She only does that when she is thinking about saying something but is unsure whether or not to say it. And as I see her do that I realize what she wants to know but hesitates to ask.

How was my visit with my father? I didn't say anything about it when I got home last night. My mother didn't press me. But I know what she is wondering. How did it go? What happened? Am I going back to see him again.

Everything about the previous day comes back in my mind like floodwater bursting through a dam. All my efforts have failed at trying to turn my confused thoughts to something else.

My mother is still looking at me. Perhaps I should

answer those unasked questions of hers. Perhaps I would—if I knew the answers myself.

So, instead of saying anything about the battle going on in my mind, I pick up my chunkey stick and twirl it between my fingers.

"I am going down to the town house," I say. I keep my voice light.

My mother smiles at that. I know what she is thinking. *Good. He is not going back to his father.*

Am I going to go back and see him again? I am not sure about that. The thoughts in my head are like a whirlwind. The only thing I can decide now is that I need to do something—anything. Then it comes to me. Chunkey. That's it! A game with my friends is just what I need to calm the storm in my mind.

"My friends Yugi and Ugama will be waiting for me there. We are going to play."

Despite my inner turmoil, I've managed to keep my face calm. As a result, my mother still looks happy and relieved.

"Come home when you are hungry," she says. "If you wish to bring your friends, they will be welcome. There will be plenty of food."

"Wado," I call back over my shoulder as I trot down the road.

CHAPTER 9

AT THE TOWN HOUSE

I am standing partway behind a big sassafras tree that rises out of an area of woods and brush at the edge of the field by the town house. I am not moving and because I am so well concealed I am sure no one has seen me.

Our town house is the most important building in Willstown. It is made of logs, like our other structures, but it is larger. In the old days such town houses always stood in the center of our villages, although then they had lower log walls with no windows and much taller roofs that were thatched with bundles of grass.

Near the town house is the ball field where our town teams play stickball against each other or teams from other villages. Those ball games are always exciting. First one side and then the other gains the ball with their double rackets, catching it in the leather webbing fastened to the end of their ball sticks. Then they try to throw or carry the ball between the standing poles that mark the goals at each side of the field, passing it back and forth, striking at one another with their sticks, blocking and tackling, attempting to trip their opponents. Only war is fiercer than our stickball games. *Waheh!*

Stickball is a game that everyone loves. The women play it as well as the men—although most men are not foolish enough to try to play the game against our Tsalagi women. Not unless they wish to lose much blood and also get their heads broken. There is no way I would ever play stickball against a group of Tsalagi women! I value my life too much. Our women are even fiercer than the men when they play stickball.

But I do enjoy playing it with other boys or even against the grown men. I have been told by some of the men that I am fairly good at playing stickball. My own two ball sticks hang on the wall above my bed. They were made by Old Turkey, the best stick maker in our town, if not the whole of our Tsalagi nation.

"My sticks have eyes," he says. "They always see the ball. All you have to do is listen to what they tell you and follow their directions."

Stickball, though, is not a game that you play every day.

You need larger teams to play it. Also when a game of stickball is played, everyone in the village wants to be able to watch it. And most days there are other things that need doing. So special occasions such as festivals are when the game is played or when a team from another village is coming to challenge.

Chunkey is different. It is always easy to find someone to play chunkey with. All you need are two people with their chunkey sticks and one chunkey stone. And, of course, the ground on which to play the game. Everyone who plays chunkey has their own pole. We make our poles ourselves, smoothing out a long stick and shaping it until it resembles a long spear. However, unlike a spear, a chunkey pole's two ends are flattened and slightly upturned.

We do not have our own chunkey stones. Those stones belong to the town. Every town has its own stones. They are kept next to the town house. The only time they would ever be removed would be if—as has happened before—the village was forced to move. Then our chunkey stones move with us. No one knows who moves them. Some say that the stones move themselves. Others say that certain elders are secretly tasked with taking care that they are brought with us. Whatever the case may be, as soon as a new town house is erected and a chunkey field has been made, within a few days those stones appear piled near the town house.

Chunkey stones are as round as wagon wheels, but much smaller. They are all two fingers broad on their edges and just the right size to pick up and then roll in an underhand motion. Our town's chunkey stones are very old. No one knows how old they are or who made them, though it is said that our great-great-grandparents played with them when they were young. The pale stone they were carved from is hard, so it must have taken someone who was very determined a long time to make them.

I look out through the screen of leaves at the five boys of around my age who are among my best friends. Usually I would be glad to see them. Just as they would be pleased to have me join them. But now I am uncertain how I will be received. I am sure that, like everyone else, they have heard about my visit with my father. That is the way gossip is. Even a fire in a field of dry grass cannot spread faster. I was seen by Tall Man, Galuloi's father. And then by that family in the wagon.

What do my friends think of me now? Will they say anything to me about it? And if they do, how will I answer? That storm in my head is turning into a tornado.

Galuloi, the tallest of the boys, is preparing the ground on which the game will be played. It is a long flat area on the other side of the town house from the ball field. It is marked off for chunkey, kept clear of all stones and vegetation, and covered with fine sand so that the poles will glide along it easily. With a smooth branch, Galuloi is smoothing out the white sand and making the surface as clean as a field covered with new snow. Galuloi is not as skinny as I am, but he is taller than me. That is why he was given the nickname of Sky.

Ugama, Soup, is helping him. Ugama, the shortest and roundest of us all, is always by Galuloi's side. The two of them are cousins and belong to the same clan. When Ugama takes his stance and then sprints forward before hurling his pole to glide it across the sand, his feet move so fast they are a blur. Because he runs so fast, he cannot stop himself easily and so always throws himself off to the side of the pit and goes rolling for a ways before stopping.

That always makes us laugh, but not that hard. When Ugama makes one of those awkward casts of his pole, it often comes to a stop right against the stone and he wins.

Equgugu, Big Owl, is rolling the chunkey stone that has been chosen for today's game back and forth between himself and his cousin, Gayusoli. Gayusoli, whose nickname means Nose, always seems to be the keenest and smartest of us. As usual, he is not doing anything much other than watching the other. Yugi, whose nickname means Nail, is the last of my friends who is here. He is busy rubbing his chunkey pole with bear oil from the bottle he keeps in his pouch, hoping that bear oil will help him make nothing but winning throws. As if that would ever happen when I was competing with him! I like Yugi the best of my friends, even though he always jokes about winning all of my marbles. Which will never happen.

Galuloi, Ugama, Equgugu, Gayusoli, Yugi. Five of my best friends.

But one of my best friends is not here. Normally there would be seven of us, counting myself.

Udagehi, Baby, is missing. He has a badly twisted ankle. He is the best hunter among us, but while hunting three days ago he had a bad fall. I heard about it when I was at the trading post picking up sugar for my mother. His ankle is not broken, but it is swollen so badly that he cannot leave his mother's house. It will be many days before he can walk without a stick and weeks before he can run.

Some believe that he brought it upon himself. I heard that said at the trading post, by one of the old men.

"That boy bragged so much about his hunting," the old man said. "He did not do the proper things when he brought back game. He did not give proper thanks. *Awi Usdi*, the little white deer who is the chief of all the animal people, heard that boy bragging. It was *Awi Usdi* who sent him that misfortune to teach him a lesson in respect."

Several people at the trading post agreed with the old man's words.

"You are probably right," my mother said. And people nodded their heads in agreement. Every Tsalagi knows that any hunter who brags and forgets to give thanks to the spirits of the animals he catches may find himself punished by *Awi Usdi*. And a sprained ankle is the lightest punishment that might be given. If a hunter continues to behave that way, the little white deer will send him rheumatism so that he cannot hold a bow or a gun.

However, I also heard it whispered by some people that there is another reason for my friend's injury.

I have a way of walking very quietly and not being noticed right away whenever I go somewhere. I stand back to observe and listen before joining in any group. I have always been that way. So I have heard things said before such gossipers have noted my presence and changed their topic of conversation.

"These accidents," another old man at the trading post whispered to his friend, "have become more common since Sequoyah came back to our nation. It makes one wonder about those markings of his. Maybe they are more than just crazy behavior. Maybe they are bad medicine, sorcery."

That was troubling. But it was not as troubling as what I heard that old man's friend whisper in response.

"Sorcery? Ah, that is even worse than selling parts of our Tsalagi homeland to the *Aniyonega*. There is only one penalty for that kind of black magic. Death!"

Those remarks made me feel sick in my stomach.

My friends have not yet started playing. That is good. It may mean that they are still just getting ready. Everyone has their own little private songs or chants that they have learned, their little rituals to help them win. Or it may be that they are waiting for me to arrive before they start. If so, that would be very good.

I step out from behind the tree. As soon as I do so, Yugi's head turns in my direction and a smile comes on to his face. Not a frown, not a look of fright.

Good.

"Osiyo, oginali," I call out to him. Hello, my friend.

"Osiyo, Uwaholi," he calls back to me.

Now all of them have turned my way. As if they have been expecting me. That, too, is good. Though I do notice something a little sour in the expression on Gayusoli's face, almost as if he is smelling something bad with that long nose of his.

"How are you all?" I ask as I walk toward them.

"Fine."

"Fine."

And so on. Which is not bad, though I notice that only Yugi says not *Osda,* but *Osdadu.* That emphasis on the end of his phrase meaning "really fine" is a much more friendly way to respond.

I am being too sensitive.

Yugi gives me a friendly push on my shoulder. "So," he says, "are you ready to lose all your clothing today?"

He is referring to the fact that wagers are often placed on games of chunkey and that people may not just lose their earrings and bracelets, but even their shirts and shoes if they are not that good at sliding their chunkey pole next to the stone.

"Hah," I say as we grasp each other's wrists in a friendly handshake. "Maybe you are the one who will return home naked today."

Of course that will not happen to either of us. For winnings in our friendly chunkey games we just use small painted sticks, each of us with a dozen or so to bet on the outcome of our contests.

"Who will play first?" Yugi asks.

Equgugu steps forward. "I challenge Ugama," he says. "Unless he is tired of always losing to me?"

"Hah," Ugama says. "It is the other way around. It is always your turn to lose to me!"

Yugi chuckles. "It is decided, then. Ugama and Equgugu."

The two friends face each other, each with his right hand behind his back.

"Odds or evens?" Yugi asks Ugama.

"Odds," Ugama says.

Yugi begins to count out loud. *"Sa, ta . . ."*

At the count of four, the two will hold out their right hands. If the total of fingers shown is an odd number then Ugama will be the one to roll the stone.

". . . tso, nu!"

The two thrust their hands forward.

Ugama has chosen to hold out three fingers and Equgugu one. A total of four.

"You see," Equgugu says, "my luck is still better than yours."

"Hah," Ugama replies. "This just means I will begin winning your sticks that much faster."

Equgugu, who is the strongest of us all, hefts the heavy chunkey stone and then rolls it as easily as if it were a white man's coin. It travels a long way down the middle of the playing ground, almost to the very end of the field before it falls over.

"Uu! Ahhey!" Yugi shouts. I agree.

It's a very good roll, a challenging one. It will take a strong throw for Ugama to send his pole gliding across the field that far. But if the throw is too hard, then his pole will continue on beyond the space marked out for the field of play. An automatic disqualification.

Ugama, though, does not appear worried at all about how difficult this might be. He takes a swift run, his feet pounding the ground. Then he casts his pole and does his usual roll. But this time instead of sprawling out at the end he actually comes up running on his feet. Impressive! Not only that, he continues running—along the edge of the playing field—and so not interfering with his throw.

"Go," he shouts at his pole as he follows it. "Go straight!"

And his pole does just that, right at the chunkey stone where it stops—*Click!*—just as its tip lightly strikes the very middle of the stone.

I am glad I am not playing against Ugama. That throw is one of the best I have ever seen anyone make! It's so good that Equgugu is standing with his eyes as wide as the night bird he is named after. He can hardly believe it. He already feels beaten.

Sure enough, when he casts his own pole it skids off to the left and goes right out of the field of play.

As Ugama collects the three sticks they'd wagered on their contest, Galuloi steps forward with the chunkey stone he's chosen. He's next in line to play against the winner. Since I arrived late, I will be last. I sit down and lean back against the wall of the town house.

With the tip of my pole, I begin scratching patterns in the dirt. Maybe this time I can make something that looks like an eagle.

Someone sits down next to me.

"It is sad about my friend Udagehi, is it not?" Gayu-soli says, leaning his shoulder against mine in a way that does not feel friendly. Also, the way he spoke those words did not make them sound like a question. But I know that I should answer him.

"Yes," I say. "That is true."

"Is it not also true that such accidents have been happening more often?" Gayusoli's tone has become accusatory.

"I don't know about that," I say, still moving the tip of my stick in the dirt.

"Perhaps you do," Gayusoli says. "Perhaps you and your father speak about such things when you visit him."

I don't know how to answer something like that. When someone says bad things about you or your family, there is no reply that you may make to change their mind. That is what my mother often says. I trust her wisdom. The best one can do is to walk away.

But I do not want to walk away. Nor do I want to argue. I came here to get away from the confusion in my mind. I came here to play chunkey with my friends. I keep scraping the tip of my pole into the ground, digging it in hard as I do so.

"Tlahhuh!" Gayusoli suddenly shouts. He leaps up, trying to back away from me so fast that he falls on his bottom. "No!" he shouts again, his face twisted with

fright as he pushes himself farther backward with his hands and feet.

The others all turn to see what is wrong.

Gayusoli is holding both of his hands toward me as if to ward me away, as he makes signs against bad magic with his fingers. His eyes are wild.

"Those, those marks," he stammers. "Look, there on the ground. Uwohali is trying to cast a spell on me!" He scrambles to his feet and runs over to the safety of his other friends who have stopped what they were doing to stare—not at me, but at the red earth in front of me.

I stand up and look down. Just as Gayusoli says, I have made marks there. I dug them so deeply with the end of my pole into the red earth that they are easy to see. I've made them without thinking. But they are not sorcery. They are just those foolish signs that were inked on the back of my sister's dolls.

Ᏸ

W

Ꮹ

Ꮂ

I look at my friends who are all still staring my way. Galuloi has dropped the chunkey stone he was about to roll. Ugama is holding his chunkey stick in front of him like a spear. Their expressions range from the terror on Gayusoli's face to the questioning look worn by my friend—if he still is my friend—Yugi. Yugi is rubbing his hands together as he always does when something has upset him. He looks almost like a raccoon washing its food.

What can I say? I have no words for this moment.

With my right foot, I wipe out those designs in the dirt. Then, without a word, I turn and walk away.

CHAPTER 10

MY MOTHER KNOWS

I am not sure how my mother does it, but she often seems to know exactly what I am thinking. So, when I come stomping into the house after my unsuccessful attempt to play chunkey with my friends, she does not ask me what is wrong.

She simply pulls back one of the chairs at the table and nods her head toward it as she wipes her hands on her apron as if dusting it off.

Sit.

Then she places a steaming bowl of succotash in front of me. It is flavored with bacon and not bear fat—since there are no longer any bears left for us to hunt. They have all been killed or driven away by the *Aniyonega*, the white men. Those bears that survived, the old people say, have all taken refuge within their stone lodge in the heart of the tallest mountain.

That is such a sad thing. The bears and the humans have always been meant to be together. One of our oldest stories tells that long ago the people were hungry and had nothing to hunt. So one whole clan of humans, the *Anitsaguhi*, got together and decided to sacrifice themselves. They turned themselves into the first bears and gave the humans permission to hunt them.

Of course, like all beings that are hunted, they only gave away their flesh. As everyone knows, when a game animal is killed, its spirit survives and it can come back to life again in another body. Still, it can be a painful thing to die. And that was a great sacrifice for the *Anitsaguhi* to make. So it can truly be said that bear meat and the bear's sweet fat is one of the greatest gifts that was ever given.

But I only think of that story for a brief moment. That is because when my nose takes in the scent of my mother's incredible succotash, that wonderful aroma drives everything else out of my mind.

I pick up the wooden spoon and taste it. Ah! My mother's blend of corn and beans—cooked with fresh churned butter, seasoned with just the right amount of black pepper—is nothing less than perfect. She plops down another dish with several round, golden brown fritters in it. Corn pone! And then, as I am stuffing the first of those corn pones into my mouth, she fills a tall mug with sassafras tea and puts it next to my bowl.

When I finish that bowl of succotash, my mother fills it a second time. And a third. I eat so much that my stomach sticks out like a raccoon's belly after it has finished robbing a goose nest. I almost eat too much—but not quite. There's room for two pieces of cobbler made with some of the dried apples that were quartered last fall and hung in strings from the rafters over the stove.

I wish I could just keep eating. I wish I could just eat and eat and not think. But I can't. And now that I've scraped the last of the cobbler from the wooden bowl, I realize, with a sigh, that none of my problems have gone away. Things are just as they were, if not worse.

I am still the son of Sequoyah, the man even my friends think is engaging in the worst sort of bad medicine.

My mother still has not said anything. But she does raise one eyebrow as she looks at me, sitting as I am with my chin on my chest and nothing but the crumbs from the big meal I've just consumed on the table in front of me.

She's ready to listen.

I'm not ready to talk about it. How can I be? I have no idea what to say. I don't even know what questions I want to ask.

I lift my head.

"Wado, agi etsi," I say. "Thank you, my mother."

I force a smile on to my face. "You are the best cook in Willstown."

That brings a smile to my mother's face, in spite of her concern. If you want to make your mother happy, tell her that you like the food she has made for you. It always works.

But now what? How long can I hold this smile before the weight of my worries pulls it back down into a frown?

I stand up.

"I . . . I am . . ." my eyes dart around the cabin.

What am I going to do? I've done all the chores that needed doing. It is not yet time to milk the cow and my mother already brought in the eggs from our hens. There's nothing in the slop bucket to feed the hogs. And I mended every place in the fences that needed work.

Then I catch sight of my cane pole leaning in the corner. "I am going fishing!"

I walk purposefully over to the pole, pick it up. I can see out of the corner of my eye that my mother is nodding.

Good, she is thinking. *His mind is on getting food, not going back again to his father.*

"Wish me luck," I say as I go out the door. "I will bring back a big fat catfish for you to fry."

"Good luck, my son," she calls after me. "I know that you will do well."

I think that she does not notice that I have neglected to take anything along with me for bait. If I was really going to try to catch a catfish, I would be taking along some pieces of cheese or scraps of meat for my hook.

Perhaps she also did not notice me pause for the briefest moment before going down the steps from the porch.

That pause was to pick up the sheathed knife that my father loaned to me from where I had hidden it just beneath the outside windowsill.

CHAPTER 11

AN UNCERTAIN FISH

I've been here by the stream long enough for the sun to pass well into the midafternoon sky. My cane pole is next to me, but the line—which has nothing but a bare hook at its end—is still wound around the pole. I've been doing something other than fishing.

And now I am thinking that, even without bait, I probably would have had better luck with my fishing pole.

Despite everything that has happened, I still long to learn things from my father. He knows so much. I want him to teach me some of those many things he knows. The useful things, that is. Not more about those markings which just cause trouble. I can't believe I was caught absentmindedly making such marks in the earth. They make no sense at all, yet I keep remembering them—like bad dreams that keep coming back. I need to get them out of my mind and concentrate on other things. That is why I have been hacking at this part of a dry pine branch with the knife my father loaned me.

I put his knife down on top of the flat stone behind me. I hold up the piece of wood in my left hand. I meant it to be a catfish. But no catfish ever looked like this. I doubt that anyone could tell which end is the head and which the tail. I sigh, hold it out at arm's length, and drop it into the stream.

Instead of being carried away, it stays there in front of me. It circles around and around in an eddy. It bobs up and down, up and down, as if it is as confused as I am about which way to go. It is not like the long stick that I see farther out in the fast water, being carried by the current. Straight as an arrow, that big stick is allowing itself to be taken downstream.

Perhaps it will float all the way to the Mississippi. Maybe it will trace the long route my father and others of our people followed by flatboat to head west. They went all that way out to what they hoped would be a new home far away enough from the *Aniyonega* to be allowed to live their lives undisturbed. What is it like out there? Aside from my father, I do not know anyone who has resettled there. Only a few of our Tsalagi people have gone out to Arkansas. Despite the hardships here, with the white men pushing in from all sides, most of us are still here in what little is left of our eastern homelands.

But can we stay here?

It makes my head hurt to think about that. There is so much pressure being put on those of us who remain here along the Little Tennessee. So little of the land that cared for us is left. What the white men now call their states of Kentucky and Tennessee, North Carolina and Georgia was once the motherland that gave us life. But every few years more has been taken as the white men have convinced—or forced—our leaders to sign their names to the papers that tear us from our land. That is why the council has agreed that from here on in any Tsalagi who signs away land without the agreement of our whole nation will be sentenced to death.

But will that stop people from doing that, from accepting gifts or believing deceitful words? And will it just all end up with not only our land gone, but also our people fighting and killing one another?

Better not to dwell on that. I need to turn my mind

to what I can do. Think about making things—even if I am not doing so well at that right now.

I look at the other pieces of pine next to me—the other awful attempts at carvings I've made this afternoon. The sun has moved the width of three hands across the sky while I've been trying to carve and all I have for my efforts are these hacked pieces of pine. Oh, and I also have this cut across my left palm where the knife slipped. It is not that deep. It stopped bleeding as soon as I picked a plantain leaf, stuck it over the cut, and squeezed it in my hand for a while. But it is a reminder of how inept I am at everything I try to do.

It was generous of my father to let me use his knife. But, then again, he is not using it. He is not doing anything other than drawing those strange shapes. Those shapes that keep coming back to my mind.

Why do nothing but troubling thoughts keep swarming around my head like gnats? I take a stick and start to draw those signs in the clay.

No! Stop that! I toss the stick aside.

I turn my attention back to my awkward carving of a fish. It's still stuck in that eddy, circling around. What is that English word I heard the missionary say a few days ago?

"Uncertain." That's it. That's what my carving is. That's what I am, too. I am uncertain now about whether or not I will ever learn anything from my father.

I reach out and push my uncertain fish into the main current. It shoots downstream. But it is still not looking like a fish. More like an overturned canoe belonging to one of the Little People.

It floats beneath a branch where a kingfisher is perching. The bird cocks its blue and white crested head to study it. But not for long.

Pathetic. Nothing like any real fish living or dead.

The kingfisher hops off the branch and flies off across the river. Its rattling call drifts back to me. It sounds as if the bird is mocking me.

Maybe I should just jump in the river and let it carry me back toward the east along with that horrible carving I just threw away.

The call of a kingfisher sounds again. But this time it is from right behind me. I turn my head so quickly to look that I almost fall over.

My father is standing there. Despite his limp, despite the fact that my ears are keener than most, he came up so silently that I did not hear a single footfall.

His kingfisher call was so perfect that it would have fooled the bird itself. Name any sound in nature. My father can mimic it perfectly. I suddenly remember that from my childhood. It is one of my happiest memories from back then.

Sequoyah smiles down at me.

He raises one eyebrow, nods his head.

Shall I sit beside you?

I move over a little.

He leans down, placing both palms on the ground. Then, in one motion, he shifts his weight to his right arm, lifts his left arm, and swings his stiff leg forward so that he ends up sitting right next to me.

He reaches across me with his left hand to pick up one of the pieces of pine I was trying to carve into a fish.

"A good start," he says.

"It is nothing," I say. "The only thing it looks like is a piece of firewood."

My father shakes his head.

"Everything is something. Just as everything has a voice. Everything talks. You just have to listen."

He holds the piece of wood up near his ear as if it is speaking to him. He purses his lips and nods. The look on his face is so funny that it makes me laugh despite myself.

"So what is it saying?" I ask.

My father lowers the piece of wood from his ear and looks at it. It seems as if he is not looking at it, but into it. Then he reaches back and picks up his knife from the flat stone.

He makes one cut, then another. The blade moves easily along the grain, shaving off little curls. The wood doesn't resist as it did when I tried to shape it. It almost seems to be helping him, giving itself to him as a shape emerges.

He pauses, studies it, turns it, weighs it in his hand. Then he begins working again, pushing the blade away with his thumb, pulling it back toward him with his strong index finger.

"Here."

I take it from his hand. It's no longer just a rough-cut piece of pine. It's a terrapin. It looks so real that it seems ready to crawl down the bank into the water and swim away.

"How did you make this?" I ask.

"I didn't," my father says. "I just let it become what its spirit wanted it to be."

He holds up the knife. "See how I hold this?" he says. "Don't just wrap your fist around it as if it is an ax."

"You were watching me?"

"For a little while. Now look. Hold it this way. It will feel right."

I take the knife from him, adjust it in my hand. And I immediately do feel the correctness of it. It's better balanced. It no longer feels awkward to me. I watched how he moved his hand as he used the knife. I think I can copy what he did.

I feel as if a bird is fluttering in my chest. My father has finally taught me something.

I pick up another of the pieces of wood I'd hacked at before. I place the blade of the knife against it.

"Turn it the other way for the first cut."

I do so and a curl of wood slides off as I press the blade forward.

"Feel the grain of the pine," my father says. "Let it guide you."

"Ah." It's just as he says. I can feel the wood cooperating with me as I cut into it. I can already almost see the shape inside it. Another terrapin? No, a rabbit. I start to dig the blade in, eager to draw that animal out, but the blade drives in too deeply and sticks.

My father touches my wrist.

"Slowly," he says. "Speed doesn't always win. You know the story of Terrapin and Fox?"

I do, but I want to hear it from his lips.

"Can you tell it to me?"

My father leans back and removes his pipe from the pouch at his waist. He slowly fills it with tobacco, packing it into the bowl with his thumb. I keep carving as he does so, slowly, just as he said.

He pulls out flint and steel, strikes a spark into the pipe and inhales. The tobacco catches fire and glows as red as sunrise. Smoke comes out of the edges of his mouth.

"Ahhh," he says. "It happened this way, so the old people say."

"Fox was boasting. He was the fastest. No one could beat him in a race.

"'I bet that I can beat you,' Terrapin said.

"Fox laughed at that.

"Terrapin said it again. 'I bet I can beat you. Let us race through the tall grass to the top of each of the seven hills. Whenever one of us reaches the top he will stand up and shout "HUT HUT."'

"'Let us race, then,' Fox said. 'And when I win I will jump up and down on you until your shell breaks.'

"'We will race tomorrow,' Terrapin said. 'I will tie a white corn shuck on my head so you can see me.'

"The next day came. They started to race. Fox

went running through the tall grass. He was sure he left Terrapin. But ahead of him, on top of the first hill, he saw Terrapin standing. It was easy to see him. He was wearing a white corn shuck on his head.

"'HUT HUT,' Terrapin shouted, and then disappeared in the tall grass.

"Fox ran faster then. But before he reached the top of the second hill, he heard 'HUT HUT.' He saw Terrapin up there with the white corn shuck on his head.

"Fox ran even faster. But before Fox reached the top of the next hill, Terrapin was already there, standing up and shouting, 'HUT HUT.'

"And so it went, hill after hill.

"When Fox got to the top of the seventh hill he was all worn out from running so hard. Terrapin was already there waiting for him.

"'I have won,' Terrapin said.

"Fox looked close at Terrapin. 'Your eyes are all red,' Fox said. 'They were not red when we started the race.'

"'My eyes are red from all the wind and dust that got in them when I ran so fast.'

"So Fox accepted that he had lost the bet. He limped back home.

"Terrapin waited until Fox was long gone. Then he stood up and shouted, 'HUT HUT!'

"And on top of every one of the other six hills another terrapin stood up and shouted back, 'HUT HUT.' They all wore white corn shucks on their heads and they all looked alike."

CHAPTER 12

MARKS IN THE CLAY

When he finishes his story, my father laces his fingers together, puts them behind his head, leans back on the moss of the stream bank and looks up at the sky. I lean back next to him, putting my hands behind my head like him. I look up at the sky, seeing a cloud that has a shape much like that of the terrapin in his story. Like all of the stories my father tells, that tale is such a good one. As I think about it, I believe that I understand its lesson. No matter how swift or strong someone may be, it's better to plan ahead and use your wits.

When did I first hear that story from him? I'm not sure. Some of my memories of that time when I was very young are confused and have been buried in my mind because they were not ones I wanted to remember. They are from that time I've already mentioned when my father drank so much. When they called him Drunken Sequoyah and our house was often filled with Tsalagi men caught in the grasp of whiskey.

What I do remember is that his stories stopped at the same time when he decided to become sober. Instead of sitting around and telling stories, he threw himself into his work of silversmithing. I missed the stories, but I did not miss the smell of whiskey on his breath.

What happened next was not better. It took him farther from us.

What next happened was the war.

I look over at my peaceful father, smiling as he looks up so intently at the clouds moving east over our heads that it seems as if he is trying to find some message in them. It is so hard for me to imagine him as a warrior, as someone fighting and killing other people. And not just any people—other Indians.

Killing Indians was what that war was about.

I'm not sure that any of our Tsalagi people expected back then that they would ever go to war again. We had made solemn promises to the Americans that we would never fight the white men again. But then a call was sent out by Gunundalegi, the One Who Follows the Ridge, one of our major leaders.

"Fighting men are needed," the Ridge said. "The Red

Stick Creeks to the south of us are fighting the Americans. The great white general of the Americans, Sharp Knife Jackson, has asked for our help. All able-bodied Tsalagi men should volunteer. If we help the Americans win this war, then they are not likely to take any more of our land."

The Ridge's words made sense. If our people were useful allies, perhaps we would be left alone by the white men. They would see us as civilized people and not savages.

So it was that many able-bodied men did join up.

I think no one would have blamed Sequoyah if he had stayed home. He was far from able-bodied. That one leg of his was so lame that he could not walk far without pain. But my father was one of the first to volunteer. Despite that leg, he could ride a horse as well as any man. He became a private in the Mounted and Foot Cherokees, a regiment of five hundred men.

My father never spoke to me about his experiences in that brief, bloody war. I wish that he would talk to me about it. I'd especially like to know about the great battle at Horseshoe Bend that ended the Red Stick War. Both of my uncles were there, too. But neither of them ever talked at length about it either.

"The sun shone that day," is the most my uncle

Red Bird would ever say whenever I asked him.

And my uncle Big Hawk just says, "It was a hard fight."

If my father did talk about it, I know he would say more than that. And he would say it well. Everyone knows how good a speaker he is. Whatever he says, he says it clearly and well. Until people became suspicious about his obsession with those strange markings, he was often asked to be an emissary and represent our people.

I look over at my father. His eyes are closed now. What is he thinking about? Is he asleep? How can he be so restful, so peaceful, when we are threatened every day by the white men who want what is left of our land.

He must know that even better than I do. After all, he was one of those chosen by our chiefs to speak for us in 1816 at the Chickasaw Council House Meeting. There our people met with the same powerful white man, Sharp Knife Jackson, who asked for our help and then said he would be our friend forever. But it seems that "forever" to General Andrew Jackson was not even three years. Despite everything my father said, despite the protests of all our Tsalagi delegates, Jackson was as hard as stone. The proposal that my father and the others were given to take back to our National Council was not in our favor. It demanded that we give up more land in Alabama.

I shake my head at the thought of General Jackson. Our people saved his life in that war against the Red Stick Creeks. But now that he is a leader of the *Aniyonega*, all he wants to do is remove every Indian from the South.

Maybe it is true what some of our Tsalagi elders now say. Maybe Sharp Knife Jackson really is the Devil, that same evil deceiver the missionaries talk about.

I am sitting forward now with my head in my hands and my eyes closed. No, no! I do not want to think of General Jackson. It is just making me sad. I don't want to think about our being driven from our homeland. I want to learn something useful from my father. Perhaps he'll show me more about carving. Perhaps . . .

"ᎫᎳ *Tsula*," my father says. "Fox."

I turn to look at him. He is no longer resting back against the stream bank with his eyes closed. He has sat up and picked up a stick. He is making marks with it in the clay of the riverbank.

"ꝺ," he says slowly as he draws a straight line down and then curves it up like a hook. *"Tsu."*

More of those strange markings? I do not need to hear more about them now. Anything but that.

"Edoda?" I say in a soft voice. "Father?"

There's no response. He just marks another shape. It is one I have seen before. The one that looks like a big English *W*. "W," he says. *"La."*

"W?" I repeat

My father grins. "Yes. Now look at this."

He makes another mark in the clay. Now there are three shapes. And to my surprise, they look familiar to me.

"Ꮳ," he says, pointing with his stick to the first one, the one that resembles a big *G*. *"Tsa."*

"W." The *W* shape again. *"La."*

"y." A mark like an English *Y*. *"Gi."*

"Ꮳ-W-y *Tsalagi?"* It's the name of our people. "ᏣᏩy," I repeat. I can actually see and hear a pattern. And for the first time I find myself getting excited about it.

"Wait," I say, putting my finger on the shape that resembles a *G*. "Isn't this one the sign, for another sound? For *"Lo?"*

My father chuckles. "Your memory is good, but your eyes are fooling you. Look."

120

Then he draws the two signs next to each other and I can see that they are alike but different.

I've picked up another stick. "Ꮹ," I say, drawing that Y shape. *"Gi."*

My father draws a sign like an upside down *J* next to it. "Ꮅ," he says. *"Li."*

"Ꮹ-Ꮅ? ᎩᎵ!" It's our word for dog. I now see it in my mind as clearly as if it was an actual picture of a dog.

I look at my father, that same quiet smile is on his lips that is almost always there. But the light in his eyes seems brighter. He can see how excited I am.

"Edoda," I say before I can stop myself, "Father! You're not crazy!"

It's a foolish thing to say, I know. But I mean something more that that. What I mean is that I now understand my father better than I have ever understood him before.

And he knows what I mean. The small smile on my father's face becomes a little broader and he nods.

"Ah," he says, "I am glad to hear that. I was worried about myself for a while."

Then he lets loose a deep belly laugh. And I am laughing with him. I wrap my arms around my father, almost lifting him off the ground. He embraces me and almost falls as he places his weight too much on his weak leg. But I hold on to him, helping him keep his balance as we stumble around together, half dancing, there on the banks of the stream, our feet making their own markings in the red clay.

We just keep laughing and laughing.

And if anyone were to see us right now they would know for sure that the both of us certainly are crazy.

CHAPTER 13

I AGREE

When we have finally finished laughing, we sit back down together on the bank of the stream. My father and I look at the shapes he drew, symbols that now talk to me as clearly as spoken words. It is hard to find words to express what is now in my heart.

Sequoyah looks over at me and nods. He knows how I feel. But we both also know what far too many others feel about the work he has been doing.

He picks up the stick that he drew those symbols with and begins to scratch it across those carefully drawn shapes in the red mud.

"We shouldn't leave these where someone may come across them. At best, it might just confuse them. At worst, it might frighten them. It might frighten them so much that they'd do something foolish."

I remember how my friends reacted.

"Hawa!" I say. "You are right."

I pick up another stick to help him. Soon every symbol has vanished back into the moist earth.

When we are done, my father smiles that gentle smile of his again at me. But this time, there seems to be something else in his expression. It is sadness.

"Do you know," he says in a soft voice, "the story of what happened before I left for Arkansas? The story of what my wife and neighbors did to save me from my. . . craziness?"

I nod my head. He is speaking of the time I have already mentioned when my stepmother and his neighbors burned his cabin and all of the markings he had made.

I nod. "Yes, I have heard about that."

"Good. Have you heard also about the way I acted that day? How I did not try to save the work I'd done? How I did not cry or moan?"

I nod my head again.

My father puts his arm around my shoulders and looks down again at the clean bank of red clay that had once been covered with his markings.

"It is hard," he said, "when people do not understand. It broke my heart to know that my own wife and my best friends thought I was crazy and that they had to save me from myself. But what good would it have done for me to weep or complain? Sometimes the face that we show the world must not mirror what we feel inside."

My father squeezes my shoulder. "I think you know that, my son. Your face is much like my own."

I nod my head a third time, knowing that my face at this moment is far.from blank, but mirroring the pride I am feeling. I have never felt closer to my father or prouder about being his son.

"There was another reason I did not mourn the loss of all that work I'd done," my father continues. His voice has changed. It's charged with excitement. "Have you ever followed a new trail and come to a place where you can go no longer? Perhaps to a river too wide to cross, a cliff too steep to climb?"

"Yes," I say, even though I am not sure what this has to do with the story.

Sequoyah slaps his hands together as if wiping dust from them and then holds out both palms. "Uh-huh! That is where I was before my cabin was burned. All the work I had done, trying to make a new shape for every word in our language, had brought me to a place where I could go no further. But when it was all burned,

125

it was as if it showed me a new path, a way that was no longer blocked. It was not all of our words that I had to make symbols for! It was our sounds!"

Now I am a little lost. And though as my father said, I am good at not showing my emotions, I do not try to hide my confusion from him.

My father sees that and nods. "I am going too fast now. Forgive me, my son." He strokes his chin with two fingers. "I need to go back in my story. Then you may understand it better. There is much to tell."

A small sound comes from the forest behind us, the snapping of a twig. It might be a deer. Then again, it might not. It might be someone following us and listening, someone looking for proof that my father truly is doing black magic. I am glad we wiped those marks from the clay before we left the river.

My father looks in the direction of that sound and shakes his head.

"But I will not tell it here. One never knows when someone may be listening." He smiles and there is certainly sadness in his smile this time. "Even though everything I have done has been meant to help our people, there are very few here who understand that. They are so lost in their fear of bad medicine and witchcraft, that they think what I am doing has hurt them."

He rolls his shoulders as if to loosen them after carrying too heavy a load and then sighs. "So let us walk on, my son, back to my wife's cabin. Are you hungry?" He pats his stomach. "I know that I am. There was a pot of squirrel stew cooking when I left home and Ahyokah was going out to gather ramps. So a fine meal should be ready by the time we get there. Eat first and then talk. Would you like that?"

I've already tasted Sally Guess's cooking, which is almost as good as my mother's. So I have no doubt that the stew will be delicious. And ramps are my favorite spring green.

I start to say yes, but my stomach growls before I can do so.

"Ah," my father chuckles, "so there are three of us who agree. You and me and your belly." He holds up a hand and I grasp his wrist. We stand there for a moment, grasping each other's wrists. And as we do so it comes to me that my life has changed. I am ready to learn whatever my father wishes to teach me. From this point on, wherever he leads, his path will be mine.

"*Osdadu*?" he says.

"*Osdadu*," I agree. It is fine.

And then, side by side, we walk together.

CHAPTER 14

LEAVES THAT TALK

Just as my father promised, the pot of stew is waiting when we reach the cabin. But not the ramps. Nor are Sally Guess and Ahyokah there. They must still be gathering those spring greens. The only one waiting for us in the cabin is Wesa, Sally's gray cat. It wraps itself around my legs as if I was its best friend.

Although I miss having those ramps, I am glad that my stepmother and sister are not here. Whatever my father wants to share with me will be told differently. If I am the only one listening, he'll be telling it just for me.

First, though, we eat. Then the two of us, our stomachs full, go out onto the porch and sit side by side. Wesa comes out to leap into my lap, curl up, and purr contentedly. I have always been liked by cats. They are another creature brought by the *Aniyonega* that we Tsalagi have taken into our lives. And in return those cats keep our houses and barns and granaries free of mice and rats.

My father takes out his pipe, carefully fills it, lights it, and lets out a long puff of smoke. He watches that smoke drift away on the breeze toward the sunset land, the same direction he traveled when he left us.

"*Edoda*," I say, "what is it like in Arkansas?"

My father nods. "Ah," he says. "In some ways, it is very good. The land by the river is good for planting. Hills there are rolling and covered with trees. It was easy to find logs to build a cabin, not like here where the best trees have all been cut. And all the animals have not yet been killed or driven away by the white men. There are big herds of deer, great flocks of geese on the lakes. And there are bears in those rolling hills. And there is plenty of room for everyone."

Then he shakes his head. "But that does not mean things are perfect there. There are other Indians who were already there, Osages. They think all of that land is their own and they resent our being there. I am afraid that if many more of our people go west, those Osages may end up fighting us. But we may have no choice. If things go as Jackson and other greedy *Ani-yonega* want, then we will have to leave our land here whether we wish to or not."

My father looks at his empty pipe, then puts it into his pocket. "That is one of the reasons I decided to go to Arkansas. I wanted to see what that land was like. I wanted to help prepare things for the rest of our people to go there if we were finally forced to leave our homeland."

I think about my father's words. I do not want to leave our home. This place is all I've ever known and like all of our people, I would choose to stay here. But what if that choice ends up being made for us?

Sequoyah looks over at me.

"Tell me," he says, "what do you want to do with your life?"

The question surprises me. I don't answer right away. I stroke my fingers along Wesa's back, feeling his purring in my hands as much as I hear it.

"I want to make things," I say.

"Ah," he says. "As do I."

I think he is about to start talking about blacksmithing or working silver. Maybe he will take me out to his shop and show me something the way he just showed me how to use that wood-carving knife. But he does not. Instead, he starts a story.

"Long ago, *Edoda*, the great Creator, made the first book. That is what some people say. Then he gave that book to us, to the Principal People. It was right that we should have that book, for we were the strongest people back then. Because we were given that book, the gift of reading and writing was ours.

"But what happened next is that a white man came along. He saw that book and he wanted it, just as the white men today still want everything that we have. That white man was not stronger than us, but he was more clever.

"'Why do you need that book?' the white man said. 'Can it help you to hunt or defend your families? It is nothing but pieces of paper and black markings that crawl across those pieces of paper like ants. Look at what I have. I have a bow and arrow. You can use it to bring home game. You can defeat your enemies with the bow and arrow. I will trade you this bow and arrow for that useless book.'

"Our people listened to that white man. They believed his words. They took the bow and arrow and gave him the book. And so it is to this day. To this day, reading and writing belongs to the *Aniyonega* and not the *Aniyunwiya*."

He pulls out his pipe, refills it with tobacco and lights it. Then he looks over it at me.

"You have heard that story?" he asks.

"Yes," I say. "I have."

My father makes a circle in the air with his pipe. "I doubt you have heard that story as many times as I have heard it. At one time or another it seems as if everyone who knows me told me that story. Each of them hoped it would prove to me how foolish I was when I said we should be able to write our own language. They all believed that reading and writing belonged to the *Aniyonega*, not to us."

He shakes his head.

"I have always listened to stories," he says. "Most stories have much to teach us. Stories can help us understand much. But some stories are like that one I just told."

"How is that, Father?"

He lifts his hand and waves away the cloud of smoke hovering in front of him. "They are not solid. Like this smoke, there is nothing to them. They were made up to explain something that could not be understood. Yet that story, even if it is one that was just made up, could have great meaning if it was told properly."

"What do you mean?"

"You simply need to add this to the story. Add to it that our people did not understand how useful books and writing could be. They did not realize that books and writing could be used to make the white man more powerful and the Indian weaker."

I think about how much truth there is in my father's words. Just last week the white missionary who wants to teach us how to read and write English told me something like that.

"Through writing," the missionary said, "words spoken long ago, when written down, will never be forgotten. We use our writing every day. We use it to make agreements with one another, to form alliances, to build great nations. Knowledge, like that in the sacred Bible can be passed from generation to generation. Such knowledge is power."

"Like you," my father continues, looking down at his broad hands as he speaks, "I have always wanted to make things. I wanted to make things that were useful, things that were beautiful. I enjoyed trading, but it did not satisfy me. That is why I turned to drawing, to working with metals. People appreciated the things I made. And that pleased me. But I was also worried about everything happening around us. Our world was changing. And it was all because of the *Aniyonega*. We had to give up more and more of our land.

"When they first came to our lands they were weak and there were few of them. We were many and strong. So we helped them, we gave them space to live, we traded with them. They brought useful things. Knives made of steel were better than those we used to make from stone and bone. Metal pots lasted longer and cooked even better than our pots of clay. The cotton and silk and wool fabrics made the best clothing we have ever seen. And the white man's animals, the horses and cattle, the pigs and chickens, they were wonderful. Before long, every Tsalagi family was raising those animals.

"Many of those white people, too, were good people, friends to us. Some even decided to become real human beings and joined our families. But then more whites came and they were not so kind. They did not want to help us or befriend us. They wanted our land and tried to push us out. That is when we began to fight them.

"We were better warriors and we won many battles. But there were too many of them. Finally, there were so many of them that we realized we could not fight them with weapons. No matter how many we killed, there were always more of them. We had to give up more and more of our land."

My father lifts his chin and turns his head toward the north.

"When I was a boy, much younger than you, the white soldiers came in and burned our towns. Thousands of homes were destroyed. All my mother and I could do was flee to the hills. I remember looking back and seeing the fire smoke rising where our home had been as my mother urged me to run faster.

"Despite their great numbers, some of our Indian cousins thought they could still keep fighting the *Aniyonega*. Tecumseh of the Shawnees and his brother the Prophet had a vision of driving out all the white people. They asked our warriors to join them in their big fight.

"Tsunu'lahun'ski was the one who answered those envoys. 'The whites are like leaves in the forest and stars in the sky,' he said. 'You may try to drive them into the sea, but without the aid of the Tsalagi. In peace we will seek a better way.'

"So, since then, that is what we Principal People have done. We have tried to live in peace with the whites. And we have accepted many useful things from them."

My father smiles as looks over at the big gray cat still purring in my lap.

"It was easy to understand how useful those things were. But some other things," he says, the look on his face becoming serious again, "were not so easy to understand."

I have heard before many of the things my father just said. But hearing all of that history from his mouth has been different. He is not just telling the story, but leading up to something more. His words thus far have been like fitting the ground to plant. Like clearing away the stones and weeds from the earth before putting in the seeds.

"I remember," Sequoyah says, his voice slower, "the first time I saw white men use their talking leaves. I was out hunting with my cousin, Agili, the one who is now chief of your town."

My father looks off into the distance as if seeing someone there. "If it was not for his being my cousin," he says, "I am not sure I would be safe here. The fact that he is now chief is one of the reasons I came back this time." He pauses and places a hand on my shoulder. "And now I see that you are another of the reasons. Because of my work, I have neglected being your father. I hope to do better from now on."

I feel a warm glow inside me when he speaks those words. *"Aho,"* I say in a soft voice as he squeezes my shoulder.

"Agili," my father says, lifting his hand from my shoulder and gesturing toward the sunrise direction where our chief's cabin is located on the other side of Willstown. "Agili, my cousin, my clan member, and my friend. He could already speak some English back then. That day as we were hunting, we came upon a campfire and a group of friendly white hunters. Agili introduced himself to them, speaking their language.

"'Hello, friend,' he said. 'I am George Lowrey and this is my cousin George Guess,' he said, using our white man names. That made them even more friendly.

"As we sat and talked with them, one of them, his name was Dee-kee, took out a small square object from his pack. It looked like a little box, but when he opened it up we realized that it was not a box at all. It was many sheets of flat white leaves sewn together. And on every leaf there were strange little markings.

"Dee-kee put his finger on one of those leaves and began to speak.

"'Those talking leaves are telling him a story,' Agili whispered to me. 'When white men want to remember something, they make those little marks on those white leaves. Then when they look at those marks, the leaves talk the exact words back to them.'

"I thought about those talking leaves for a long time. If the white men could do such a thing, I should be able to do it, too. That was when I first began to try to use markings to hold words. Back then, our people would often come to my store to get things and then pay me for them later. It was not easy to remember everything they got. I saw how being able to hold on to memories without having to remember them in my head would be useful to a storekeeper such as myself.

"So I began making talking leaves of my own. I drew pictures of each of the people who traded with me on credit. Then beside their pictures I made marks to keep track of what they owed. I drew circles and lines that had different meanings for me. A big circle would mean a wagon wheel. A small circle would mean a cheese. A small thin line could stand for a needle while a big thick line could stand for an axle. A half circle was a horseshoe, while a curved line meant a scythe. It was all I could think about.

"At night I lay awake trying to think of other shapes and signs that could stand for things I sold such as packages of buttons and bolts of cloth. A button could be a small circle. But what if some of those buttons were made of glass and were more expensive while others were made of bone and were cheaper? How could I draw the difference with a simple shape? And what if some of the bolts of cloth I sold were blue and more costly than the cloth that was white?

"All of my circles and lines and other shapes helped, but I could not find a system that would work for everything. I grew more and more frustrated. Instead of paying attention to my customers, I spent my time trying to invent shapes that would stand for the items I sold while also being easy and quick to draw. Sometimes those who came to pick up things from my store would mutter under their breath about the way I was acting. Some would tap their heads and look at me with pity. Some looked worried and left without buying anything. I paid no attention to them. I had to figure out something. But I still did not know what that something was.

"One night I went to visit my cousin Agili. We sat outside with some friends around a fire.

"'The *Aniyonega* have great magic,' I said. 'They can make leaves that talk.'

"'That is true,' one of the men said. 'We can never match them.'

"'No,' I said. 'That is not true. We can have our own talking leaves.'

"'Yes,' Agili said, 'Sequoyah is right. It is possible for us to learn to speak English. The missionaries can teach their writing to you, just as they taught it to me. They tell us English is much better than Tsalagi and I think they may be right. We need to forget Tsalagi and just use English. Then when we know English well enough, we can write as they do and make our own talking leaves.'

"Agili thought he was agreeing with me, but he was not.

"'No,' I said. 'No, no! That is not what I mean. I do not want to give up our own language. I want to do this in Tsalagi.'

"I did not want to give up our language for English. That is why, though I can understand some of the white man's tongue, I have never truly learned to speak or write it. I love our beautiful language, the language of our grandparents, of our stories and songs. It is the language of the land itself, as musical as the singing of the birds and the wind in the trees. It seemed to me that if we forgot our language, we would forget how to be Tsalagi people. We would gain knowledge but lose ourselves. If we were to read and write, we needed to

140

do it in our own way. English was too hard. Tsalagi is the language we talk in. It is the language we think in. We needed to be able to read and write Tsalagi. Then everyone in our nation would be able to learn it. With such reading and writing we could rebuild our nation and keep it strong. We would not have to rely on the white men to keep track of our dealings with them. We could send messages back and forth to one another. We could hold on to our histories and our stories and we would do so not in the language of our enemies, but in our own tongue and in our own way.

"But back then, no one agreed with me. In fact, my friends looked at me as if I was insane.

"'Sequoyah, that is not possible,' Agili said.

"'No, no,' I said. 'Look.'

"Then I took a pin from my headcloth. I picked up a flat stone.

"'Watch,' I said, 'I will make a word.' I scratched a picture of a bird with the pin. 'You see,' I said. 'What is this?'

"'*Tsisqua*,' one of my friends said.

"'Of course,' I said. 'See how easy it is!'

"But Agili shook his head. 'Cousin, what kind of bird? Buzzard? Hummingbird? And what is it doing? Is it flying? Is it eating? Is it a dead bird or is it alive?

And what if it was a flock of birds? Would you draw all of them.'

"They all laughed at that. And I had to agree. They were right. It was not as easy as just drawing pictures.

"I said no more about it that night. I just sat there in silence next to that fire and listened as the talk turned to other things. Agili and my other friends thought I had given up on my foolish idea."

"This all happened many years ago. In the years that followed, many of our people did what my cousin Agili had done. They learned to read and write English."

My father looks at me. "You have, but that was not the way I chose. It was hard, but I did not give up. There had to be some way to make marks that could be understood as easily as white men understand English writing. Perhaps I could even find a way to make marks that would be easier to understand than the English way of writing. But I did not yet know how to do it."

◇✕◇✕◇ CHAPTER 15 ◇✕◇✕◇

GOING TO WAR

My father has been silent for longer than usual. The look on his face has changed. It is as if a cloud has come across it. Then he lets out a long sigh.

"The Horseshoe," he says.

I do not understand. I lean forward. "You want me to get a horseshoe."

A brief smile moves across his lips. "No," he says. "I have come to a trail that is hard for me to follow. It is hard to talk about. But you should know this darker path, a bloody path that led to war, because it is part of my story."

"Uh-huh," I say because now I understand. My father is speaking of Horseshoe Bend, that place along the Tallapoosa River where the Cherokees fought by the side of the *Aniyonega* in a great battle against other Indians during what was called the Red Stick War. I have often wanted to hear about that, but none of my elders who fought there ever wanted to talk about it.

My father pauses to tap out his pipe. He slips it into his pocket, his gaze and his memory reaching far away and looking back in time.

I bite my lip and wait for his words. And when they finally come they do so as slowly as the first drops of water released by a bank of snow touched at last by the sun.

"First I must tell you this story," he says. "It is not a tale from ancient times. It was seven years ago, a dangerous time for all of our Indian nations here in the South. It was not just Tecumseh and his Shawnees who had visions of driving away the white men. Among our own people, a medicine dance took place at Utsanali. A Cherokee man—whose name is best forgotten—said he was a prophet and that he had been given a great vision by the Creator. All of the bad things that had come to us were caused by the white man. To change our fortune there was only one way to go. We had to stop using all of the things that came from the white man. Our Tsalagi people had to take off their white man's clothing, burn their own

144

houses and their own mills. They were told to burn their beds and chairs and tables—because we had no such things in the old days. They were told to abandon their beehives and their orchards, and kill their cats. Then they had to put on red paint and deerskin clothing and climb to the top of the highest mountain peaks to wait. A great flood would come with the full moon and wash into the sea all of the white people and the Indians who followed them.

"Many of our people believed that false prophet. They did as he told them to do. They burned or just abandoned their homes. They made the long hard climb to those high places. But when the full moon came, there was no flood. Nor did one come the day after that. Finally, hungry and discouraged, the people returned sadly to what was left of their homes. Giving up those material things that came from the white people, things that had made their lives easier and better, had not helped them at all."

My father looks over at me, one eyebrow raised. He raises his eyes up as if to look at the turban wrapped around his head, looks down at the shirt he is wearing made of trade cloth, then looks over at me as if studying my own clothing.

"Who made this clothing that we wear?"

145

"The *Aniyonega*," I reply.

"Does wearing these clothes make us white men? Do we need to give them up to be who we are?"

I see what he means. It is not what we wear or the things we use that make us Tsalagi. We can accept many things from the white people, make those things our own and still stay true to ourselves.

"No," I say.

My father smiles. Then he continues his story.

"Among the towns of the Muskogee Creeks who lived to the south of us along the Tallapoosa River, there were people who believed a similar sort of foolishness—just like those of our people who burned their own houses and killed their cats A prophet had risen up among them, too. That prophet also said they had to give up the things that came from the white men. However, that Muskogee prophet went even further. His vision was not one in which the white people would be washed away by a flood. Instead, he spoke of weapons and rivers of blood. He told his people that they had to kill all the white men or push back into the ocean.

"The Upper Muskogee Creeks sent envoys to the Tsalagi, asking us to join them. But just as we had refused Tecumseh's offer, our council turned them down. War against the *Aniyonega* would only lead to our own destruction. We had pledged to never again fight the white men and we would never break that pledge.

"Not all of the Muskogee Creeks wanted war, either. Those in the Lower Creek towns knew that fighting against the white men would probably result in their own destruction. They said it was foolish to give up the useful new things that had been brought by the whites. The argument between the Upper and Lower Creeks became heated. Soon a war began between the Upper and Lower Creek nations. Indians were killing one another and many died.

"The Upper Creeks were strong and they were winning that war against their brothers. They felt so powerful that they decided it was time to wipe out the white men who lived nearby. Led by their chief Weatherford, the Upper Creeks, who were now known as the Red Sticks, attacked the white fort on the Tensaw River, overwhelmed and destroyed it. Five hundred white soldiers and settlers died there. The only ones spared were a few people who were of Indian blood and some of the black slaves. It was a great victory for them. But the white men called it a massacre. And so it was in

August of the year the white men call 1813 that they joined in the war as the allies of those Lower Creeks and their chief McIntosh.

"That was when my cousin Agili and my friend Turtle Fields came to see me. It was clear from the packs they carried and the muskets they had with them that they were getting ready to set out somewhere.

"'The Ridge has sent out a call for men,' Agili said.

"'Our chief Pathkiller asked him to do this,' Turtle said.

"'Sharp Knife Jackson is leading the Tennessee Militia to war against the Red Stick Creeks. He is asking all the loyal Indians to join him,' Agili said. 'If we do so, then he will see what useful allies we are. He will surely show his friendship to us by supporting us when others of the *Aniyonega* try to take more of our land again.'

"'Those Red Sticks have already killed some of our Tsalagi people,' Turtle said. 'That is another reason for us to fight them.'

"'We will not be alone,' Agili added, with real emotion in his voice, 'There are Choctaws and Chickasaws and many of the loyal Creeks who are going to join Sharp Knife's army. You must join us, cousin. This will be a good thing.'

"I did not stop to think. The words my friends spoke sounded right to me at that time. None of us realized what a liar Jackson would prove to be and that his promises of friendship to our people meant nothing. And back then, even before he became a village chief, my cousin Agili was very good at persuading people to do things.

"'My friends,' I said, 'I will go with you.'

"Why did I do this? There were many reasons, I suppose. I wanted to help my friends. Any man who has been to war will tell you that it is more about staying by the side of your friends than it is about trying to win great battles. You do not fight and die for your leaders, but for your brothers, the men beside you. I suppose it is also true that I wanted to prove myself. I might have been lame, but I was as good as any man with two good legs.

"But there was, to be honest, another reason. All I had been able to think about for so long was finding a way to write our language. Perhaps, if I went to this war, I would somehow find the answer in my mind to that question which kept me awake at night, that question of how to make shapes that would talk in Tsalagi. Perhaps, too, a part of me thought that going to war might help me escape from my obsession. It might free my mind from the confusion that had settled around me like a cloud.

"I remember how your mother watched me as I did so. She had been listening to my conversation with Agili and Turtle and knew what was happening. There was a resigned look on her face. She did not ask me to stay or encourage me to go. She just said nothing. In truth, I think she was just as glad to see me go. I had not been a good husband. My drinking and strange ways had been hard on her. Although your mother told me that our marriage was over after I returned, I think she had already made that decision on the day I left for the war.

"I remember, too, how you behaved that day I left. You did not cry, but you held on to me so hard that it was difficult to make you let go."

My father reaches out his left hand, the one closest to his heart, and rests his palm for a moment on my chest. I feel a lump in my throat and swallow hard.

"Maybe you have heard stories about war, about bravery and great deeds. Those tales do not tell you what war is really like. They do not talk about the smell of battle, what it is like to see a man you know trying to keep his intestines from coming out of a great wound in his belly. Those stories do not tell you how terrible it is to cause the death of an enemy, a person who is just as much a human being as you are.

"My friends and I agreed to serve in that army for only three months. That may not seem long. It is only a little more than the time it takes to plant your corn and bring in the crop from the fields. But those three months were long and hard. And the harvest we brought in was death and destruction.

"The Red Stick Creeks were brave fighters. In battle they would never surrender but fight to the last man. They were so fearless in battle that they frightened the white men. Many of Jackson's white soldiers ran away. In one battle his whole Tennessee Militia ran all the way back to the Coosa River as we Indians fought to cover the retreat. If it had not been for our regiment, the Mounted and Foot Cherokees, Sharp Knife would have lost his own life. By the end of that year, nearly all of Sharp Knife Jackson's white soldiers had deserted or served out their terms and gone home.

"When our own term of enlistment ended, we, too, could have gone home. But we did as almost every other Indian did. We re-enlisted. Sharp Knife brought in new white recruits. Our army grew in size. Soon, counting our five hundred Cherokees, it numbered more than two thousand.

"And that was our strength in March of 1814 when we came to Tohopeka, the place the white men call Horseshoe Bend."

CHAPTER 16

HORSESHOE BEND

My father levers himself up from his chair. He shakes his lame leg and stomps it twice on the floor before putting his weight onto it. Then he walks toward the steps.

"Come," he says, his hand brushing my knee.

And though Wesa protests as I gently push him out of my lap, I stand up, too. I follow my father as he makes his way down the steps, walks around the front of the cabin, and starts across the backyard.

He does not go far. A stone's throw from the cabin are two stumps next to each other. In front of those stumps is a patch of clear ground where the loose, sandy soil is as smooth and unmarked as a baby's face. And next to each stump is a small, thin pole with the bark peeled from it. I am not sure what those poles are for. But they look as well used as ball sticks or farm tools.

My father limps over to sit on one of those stumps. He pats the one next to it and I take a seat there. He carefully picks up the smooth stick closest to him and holds it between his thumb and his first two fingers the way I have seen the missionary hold a pen.

"Here," he says. He begins to scratch shapes in the smooth soil with the tip of the stick.

For a moment I think he is making more of those symbols that stand for sounds. But then I realize that what he is drawing is something other than that. It is a map.

"North," my father says, tapping the top of his drawing. "South," placing his stick down near the bottom. "The Tallapoosa River," he continues, following a line he's made that comes curving down from the northeast, then takes a sharp bend up, down, and around. Its shape is that of a horseshoe.

He leans back, takes a breath. Then he leans forward again and holds his drawing stick above that peninsula of land formed by the river. "This is where the Red Sticks made their final stand," he says. "They had a thousand warriors there at Tohopeka within a hundred acres of land."

With the point of the stick he draws lines across the neck of the peninsula.

"They built walls of logs across the entrance. They were taller than a man, and so thick that even cannon fire could not break them down. They slanted in so that anyone coming close could be shot at from two sides. The Red Sticks behind that wall all had muskets and plenty of powder and balls, as well as bows and quivers full of arrows."

He taps his stick behind the wall. "Their houses were back here. Their women and children were there. Three hundred of them. So, of course, their men fought harder to protect them."

He moves the stick to the bottom of the peninsula. "And here is where they had placed their canoes along the river, so they could use them to escape if necessary."

My father begins making shapes like small crosses along the opposite banks of the river surrounding that peninsula. "This is where we were, the mounted white men and almost all the Indians. We surrounded them before the fight started."

He draws two circles in front of the neck of Tohopeka. "And this is where Sharp Knife Jackson was with his cannons."

A little smile comes to my father's face.

"Do you know who was with Sharp Knife that day? My white friend, Big Drunk, drinking from the jug he had in his pack."

That brings a smile to my face, too. Of all the white men who have spent time among the Tsalagi, Big Drunk is our favorite. He's a tall, broad man, generous and kind. Our people adopted him when he was a boy, and gave him the name of Golanu, the Raven. His one weakness is his constant drinking and the source of his nickname Big Drunk. We hardly ever call him by his *Aniyonega* name of Sam Houston.

My father's face grows serious once more. "When the battle started that wall of logs held. The fire from inside the barricade was so fierce that every time the militia men tried charging the wall they were driven back—with musket bullets flattened on their bayonets."

He points to the right side of the river across from the lower part of Tohopeka.

"I was here. We were firing across the river at the Red Sticks defending its banks. Word came down to us that the fight was not going well. Perhaps the white troops would give up and run from the battle as they had done before. That was when we Indians knew we had to take our fight to the other side of the river.

"'There are plenty of boats,' I said. 'There on the other side. Follow me.' Then I walked into the river.

"I cannot run fast with this leg, but I have always been a good swimmer and so I was not afraid of the water. The current was not strong there and in some places there were sandbars we could walk upon. It was easy to reach that other side—aside from all the bullets that were striking the water around me and the other men who followed me. We held our rifles and our powder above the water. So, when we got to the other side, we started shooting back at the Red Sticks guarding the riverbank. Others of us took the Red Stick canoes and paddled them over to ferry back more men.

"It was hard fighting, but we pushed the Creek warriors back toward the wall. We got there just as Sharp Knife ordered all of his men to charge from the other side. I reached the wall in time to see that one of the first to climb over the barricade was my friend Big Drunk. He looked very angry. One of the Red Stick musket balls had broken his whiskey jug."

Once again that little smile lights up my father's face, but it vanishes just as quickly as the sun disappearing when a dark cloud crosses over it.

"Many things happened fast then," my father says. His voice is strangely calm. "You'd think it would be hard for me to remember it all."

He shakes his head. "But it is the other way around. I do not think I will ever forget any of it. Sometimes when I close my eyes, I am back there again. People are screaming and shouting, I hear the whistling of arrows past my head, the sound of bullets thudding into bodies. And I smell the thick stench of guts and blood—like hogs being butchered.

"It was hard for me to stand. That was not because of my bad leg. The earth was slick under my feet with the blood of men, most of them Red Sticks. They lay everywhere around me, piled like cornstalks flattened by a great wind. Some called for water or spoke the names of their loved ones with their last breaths. I can hear them even now."

My father lifts up the stick with which he was drawing out the lines of battle.

"Not one Red Stick surrendered. When it was done and the bodies were counted, there were exactly five hundred and fifty-five dead Red Stick warriors there inside their fort. Some managed to reach the river, but their canoes were gone. All they could do was try to swim. A few got away. But most were shot or drowned as they tried to escape. Three hundred prisoners were taken, but only three of them were men.

"On our side, eighteen Cherokees and five Creeks were killed and twenty-six Americans. That was all. Sharp Knife and his officers were pleased. It was a great victory, they said. We were praised for all that we did to win the battle for them."

My father rubs two fingers across his chin.

"Praised," he says. "Hah! That praise did not keep other American soldiers from pillaging our villages while we were away. We came home to find all our livestock gone, our stores of food stolen, and many of our houses burned. Sharp Knife said he was sorry that happened, but seven years have now passed and we have yet to see the money he promised to pay us for our losses."

Sequoyah taps the end of the stick on the map he drew in the soft soil.

"A great victory," my father says. "A great victory. Those were the words of Sharp Knife Jackson. But it was not that. It was a slaughter there in that bend in

159

the river. I had escaped without being struck by any musket ball or arrow shot by an enemy's hand. I was unwounded in my body. But not in my spirit."

My father reaches his hand up to wipe his eyes. Then he leans down, using his hands to support himself as he goes to his knees. Then, with his left hand, he begins to carefully wipe away all trace of the map he had drawn. It takes him some time before the earth is smooth and clean again. But even though the shapes of that terrible battle have been removed from the soil, I know they will always remain in his memory. Just as they will now surely remain in mine. Never again will I be able to think of war without remembering his story or the horrors he saw at the Horseshoe.

He dusts the earth from his hands and shakes his head. Then he holds out his right hand to me and I help him rise to his feet. The two of us sit back down again on the stumps. We stay there in silence for a long time. Somewhere off in the trees I can hear the drumming of a pileated woodpecker as it hammers its beak against a tree. The warm wind, coming as soft as a mother's hand to caress our faces, begins to dry the tears on my father's cheeks . . . and on my own.

"When I came home," my father finally says, "something had changed in me. I had made the mistake of thinking I could be a warrior. But that was not who I was or ever again should be. I would never again go to war—not for the *Aniyonega* or for my own nation. I would never kill another human being or take part in the killing. But more than that had changed in my mind and in my heart. Although those false prophets and the Red Sticks who followed them were wrong in most things, I now knew how right they were in wanting to stay true to who they were, in wanting to stay Indian.

"After that experience of war, I knew what I had to do. Before, I had been obsessed with the idea of finding ways to make symbols I could use in my store. Now it was much more. It was not just for myself, but for all our Tsalagi people. It was as if a fire was burning in my heart. Learning how to write our language was the way I could help our people. It could help us be stronger, help us remain Tsalagi. It could help bring us together, help us find peace."

"I understand," I say. And as I say it I realize that it is not just that I finally understand my father and what he wants to do. It is not just that I feel closer to him. It is as if some of that fire is now burning in my own heart as well.

We're no longer alone. From the nearby house we hear the sound of people talking. Then a child's voice calls out.

"Father, where are you? We are back and we picked many ramps! Mother is cooking them."

It is, of course, Ahyokah.

My father nods. He lifts his hand and wipes his face. Then he stands up.

"Time to eat ramps," he says.

CHAPTER 17

86 SYMBOLS

My father is quiet as we walk back to the house. Even when Ahyokah comes running up to grasp his hand, the thin smile he gives her does not extend beyond his lips. The darkness of that bloody memory is still there behind his eyes. His talking about the Red Stick War helped bring me close and understand him. It was a gift to me, but it was also painful for him to do.

As we sit together at the table, enjoying those fresh, steaming ramps, I look across the table at my father. That little smile is wider on his face now. He nods at me.

"The ramps are good," he says.

"Yes," I say, and smile back at him as I do so.

When we have finished eating, Ahyokah turns to her mother.

"Can we show my brother now?" she says.

"Perhaps your father is too tired?" Sally Guess says. I can tell by the tone of her voice that she is teasing.

"Mother!" Ahyokah says.

"All right, my stubborn child. Ask your father."

Ahyokah looks toward my father. He already has one hand raised up, palm outward. "I surrender," he says. "I am your captive and I must do as you say."

"Good!" Ahyokah declares. "I will go get it."

She jumps up from the table and runs over to a chest on the other side of the room. Meanwhile, my father brings a goose quill pen and an inkwell to the table. In two shakes of a deer's tail, Ahyokah is back, a small stack of papers in her hands that she plops down on the table in front of us. I note that those sheets of paper are blank, except for the one that he places in front of me.

I immediately recognize what is drawn there, even if most of it makes no sense to me. There are those shapes he showed me, the ones that stand for the sounds of *Tsu*, *Tsa*, *La*, *Gi*, and *Lo*. But there are dozens of other shapes as well, neatly arranged in several columns.

Ahyokah is so excited she can barely contain herself.

"See them all?" she says.

"Yes, I do."

"Do you know how many there are?"

"No."

"Well, I do. And I know them all. Listen"

Then, placing her finger on each symbol in turn, she begins to recite in a high, clear voice.

"*Da, Ga, Ka, La, Ma, Na . . .*" she reads. Reads! That is it, isn't it? As she continues, my mouth is shaping what she is saying silently. But what is it that she is saying? It doesn't make any sense. I look up at my father and he looks back at me with one eyebrow raised, a look that means *think*.

I try to do that. Every sound she makes seems as recognizable to me as the call of a familiar bird. Then I realize—just as I should have realized from the start— what she is doing. Ahyokah is not saying words.

My sister is reading the sounds of the Tsalagi language.

Sequoyah sees the look of understanding that has come over my face and nods his head.

As Ahyokah continues to read I am counting the different sounds. Five, six . . . she finishes one column, begins the next, and then the next. Fifteen, sixteen . . . on and on. Fifty, fifty-one . . . more and more. Eighty-three, eighty-four . . . Finally she speaks the last two symbols, the one that resembles an English number six, "*Wu*," and the one I have seen before that looked like a capital *B*, "*Yu*." Eighty-six markings. Eighty-six sounds.

So many! I'm amazed. I think she has just read every sound in our Tsalagi language.

My little sister looks up at me and smiles. "You see?" she says.

I am so excited that it takes all my effort to breathe and make my mouth move. "Yes," I say. "I do see. I do."

And that is true. Though my father has not yet explained it completely to me, I believe I understand what can be done with these symbols that represent all the sounds of Tsalagi. If you put them together in the right order you can do more than say anything.

You can also write anything.

It is like magic. But it is not really magic of any kind, neither black nor white. It is no more magic than the writing of the *Aniyonega*. But it is powerful. It is power.

I look over at my father for permission to take that paper from Ahyokah's hands. He nods at me. I hold my hand out toward my little sister.

"Here, brother," she says, handing me the sheet without any hesitation. My hand is trembling as I reach out. Ahyokah's eyes meet mine as I grasp that sheet of paper. I read the question in her expression.

166

Are we in this together now?

I bite my lip and nod back at her.

I feel as if everything, everything in my life is going to be different from this moment on.

I study the sheet of paper and its powerful markings carefully. Each symbol is clearly different from every other one. They look as if they would be easy to draw, as well, even by someone not as great an artist as Sequoyah.

"Has my sister learned how to use these?" I ask.

My father nods. "It took her some time, but she is perfect at them now. She can both write and read them. Watch."

He turns to my little sister. "Are you ready?"

Ahyokah nods, the smile on her face even bigger than before.

"Then go outside and wait for me to call you."

She walks out the door and sits down on the top step, her back still visible but out of earshot.

"Now," my father says, "whisper something slowly to me."

I lean close. "My name is Uwohali. I am the son of Sequoyah. I am sorry I thought my father was crazy. My little sister knows more than I do."

"Good," my father says, the pen in his hands moving as smoothly across the paper as a fish swimming through clear water, pausing only when he dips the goose quill into the ink. I am not whispering all that slowly, but the symbols easily keep up with my words.

"Is that all?" my father asks.

"Yes, no, wait. Write this on the other side." I whisper another few words that bring a smile to Sequoyah's face and a chuckle from Sally Guess, who has now come to stand behind his shoulder. He turns the paper over to the other side, adds more symbols there, and then puts down the pen.

"Come back in," my father calls.

Ahyokah darts in, as quickly as Wesa catching sight of a mouse. She takes the paper from my father's hand and reads it aloud, saying exactly what was written on the front of the page.

"'My little sister knows more than I do,'" she reads. Ahyokah looks up at me, a smug smile on her face. "Yes, I certainly do," she says.

"There is more," I say. "Look at the back."

Ahyokah turns the sheet over. The self-satisfied look on her face turns into a gasp as she drops the paper to swat at her right shoulder.

"Oh!" she says. "Oh! Uwohali, you are a bad big brother. There is NOT a big black spider on my right shoulder!"

She pokes me in the stomach with her hard little fist. I hug her as we both dissolve into laughter, joined by my father and Sally Guess.

Within this family I cannot think of a time when I have felt happier. But I know there is one thing that will make me happier still. When we have all stopped laughing, I pick up the first sheet of paper, the one paper marked with those eighty-six perfectly drawn symbols that stand for the sounds in our beautiful language.

"Will you teach me?" I ask my father.

"I've already begun," he replies.

CHAPTER 18

YUGI'S WARNING

I am floating down the river. The current is moving swiftly, carrying me along toward the rapids, but I am not worried. It is not just because I am a good swimmer. It is because I am with my father.

He nods at me and I nod back at him.

The two of us are going west in this boat, leaving behind the homeland of our people, heading for a new place to live. I am sad to leave behind our old lands, but I am also hopeful. We may be safe there. Perhaps we will be so far away from the white men that they will not follow us and try to drive us from our new land.

I also am not worried because my father and I have faith in this strong boat that is carrying us along. It is like no boat I have ever seen before, but I know why it is so strong. It is not made of wood, but Tsalagi words. All of those words have been written in those symbols that my father has been teaching me to write. Those syllables are braided together like ropes, wrapped tightly into strong bundles. And those syllables are much more than drawn shapes. They are voices, breathless voices whispering encouragement to us.

We will remain together, they whisper.
We will be strong.
We will be Tsalagi
We will never forget who we are.

Then something hits the side of the boat. It's a stone. Someone is throwing stones at our boat. I can't see who it is, but I can hear those stones striking.

Tink! Tink!

I have to see who it is. I turn my head and . . .

I find myself sitting up in my bed, rubbing my eyes. The river and the boat made of words are both gone. The only sign of those symbols I have been practicing writing is the piece of paper I left on the windowsill and the bit of charcoal I've been writing them with. I had meant to hide them away so that my mother would not see them, but I was so tired last night that I forgot.

I swing my feet onto the floor.

Tink!

Tink!

Small stones are not hitting the side of that boat in my dream, but the wall of my mother's cabin beside my window. I get up and look out.

Someone is standing out there, a stone's throw away. He is half concealed in the bushes on the other side of our garden. He is waving his arm at me now that he has gotten my attention. He leans to the side and his face is visible. I recognize him.

It's my best friend—or at least the one who used to be my best friend. Yugi.

I motion for him to come to me. He shakes his head and then points with his chin toward the woods. There's a place there where the two of us used to play together.

Come, he motions to me and then drops back down out of sight to crawl away.

I think I understand why Yugi is behaving this way. Over the last several days I have been spending more and more time with my father. And I have heard people talking. The things they said about my father are now being said about me as well. People are suspicious, even angry. All of my friends have been staying away from me. No one likes to be talked about behind their back, even when that talk is about harmless things. But when the talk is about bad medicine, about witchcraft—ah, ah! That is terrible.

Now, even to be seen speaking with me in a friendly way might start others talking about him that same way.

Where Yugi hid in those bushes, he could not be seen by anyone who might be walking or riding along the road in front of my mother's house. It was still a risky thing for him to do, to wake me this early to call me out to meet with him. It may mean that, despite it all, he is still my friend.

I dress quickly.

My mother is already up.

"Where are you going?" she asks.

"Yugi," I say. "I am going to meet him at the Four Bears."

"Are you sure?" she says. She, too, has been hearing what people are saying and it has worried her. She has not told me to avoid my father. But she has been urging me to be careful.

"I trust Yugi," I say. "He would never do anything to bring harm to me."

My words are more certain than my thoughts, but they mollify my mother.

"Go then," she says. "But eat something first."

I take the bowl with several corn pones in it and the cup of buttermilk she hands me. I also take a piece of charcoal from the fireplace and put it into my pocket.

As I follow the path that leads to the Four Bears, I think about how often in the past my friend Yugi and I have met there. None of our other friends know about the spot. Yugi and I found it together three years ago. It was such a special place that we decided to keep it our secret. As far as I know, my mother is the only other person who knows where it is. She is the one who told me about its location because it was her special place when she was a little girl.

I turn at the head of a steep ravine where a stream has cut down through the hills. It's not an easy trail to follow. Instead, I duck my head under a tangle of blackberry canes and enter a hidden gap between the stones of the hill. A few blackberry leaves have fallen on the ground of our secret path. Still green, just broken from the canes, they are a sign that some-one has already pushed through ahead of me.

The passageway formed by the gap between the stones and earth of the hill is almost like a tunnel or the entrance of a cave, though there is a narrow strip of light overhead. Another turn and the passageway opens out into a space the size of a small room. Half of the space is taken up by the four big red stones that look a little bit like four-legged figures. The Four Bears is what we decided to call them. Yugi is sitting where he always sits, leaning back against the first of those stones.

He usually teases me about how long it takes me to catch up with him. He jokes that my nickname should be Turtle rather than Eagle because I am so slow. But not today. His face is too serious for any teasing.

"*Siyo*, Yugi," I say. Hello.

"*Siyo,*" he answers. Then he looks down at his long, slender hands. He's rubbing them together as he al-ways does when he is nervous.

I sit down next to him.

"It is good to see you, my friend," I say.

Yugi does not answer. He just keeps rubbing his hands together.

Silence can be companionable. But not this sort of

silence. It makes me want to shout at him. Shout what? I don't know. I bite my lip.

"The things," Yugi says, his voice very soft, "the things they are saying. Those things are not good."

"What things? Who?"

More rubbing of his hands. I want to grab them and make him stop that. But instead I fold my hands together and wait.

"It is Gayusoli," Yugi finally says. "He says that you have become as bad as your father. He says that it was you who caused Udagehi to have his accident. His father says that Sequoyah and anyone helping him should be driven away. Anyone helping him—that is you."

I swallow hard. It is difficult to hear that one of my best friends is now so fearful of me. I wonder how all this could happen so quickly? But even as I wonder that I know the answer. Our Tsalagi people have always been worried about witchcraft, fearful that it might be used to injure them or their families. Such fears have grown worse in recent years, perhaps because of all the pressure that the *Aniyonega* are putting on us. When they do not understand something, far too many of our people now are quick to believe the worst.

I open my mouth to say something, but Yugi stops me by raising his hand.

"Wait," he says. "There is more I must tell you. What Gayusoli's father says is not as bad as what others are talking about. Listen. This is what I heard myself just yesterday at the trading post. There was a group of men in the corner with their heads together. One of them was Sharp Teeth, the father of Udagehi. They looked so serious that I decided to try to listen in to what they said. I did as I have seen you do, Uwohali. I pretended not to listen while I was listening.

"'It has gone too far,' Sharp Teeth said.

"'You are right,' another man agreed. 'First your son is hurt. Then my cow stops giving milk. It is witchery for sure. It is Sequoyah's doing.'

"'What shall we do?' a third man asked.

"Udagehi's father began nodding his head. 'What was done before,' he said. 'Remember when the cabin of Sequoyah was burned with all of his witch markings in it.'

"'Yes,' the second man said, 'but will that be enough?'

"Sharp Teeth smiled then. It was not a good smile to see. 'It will be enough,' he said, 'if this time Sequoyah— and his son and daughter—are in the cabin when it is burned.'"

Yugi stops talking. There's fear in his eyes and I wonder if it is fear about what might happen to me or fear of me. Does he think I am really engaged in black magic? A chill goes down my back. Things are even worse now than I had feared. I'm finding it hard to get my breath. Our own people now wanting to harm us because they are afraid of my father's writing? How can people be so foolish?

Yugi wipes his mouth with the back of his right hand. It's as if he is trying to get rid of the taste of the words he just spoke. And all of a sudden, strange as it is, I find myself feeling more sorry for him than worried about myself.

Perhaps it is because I can see that he is confused. I am not confused anymore. Nor, I realize, am I frightened.

"Yugi," I say, "*Wado*, my friend. Thank you for warning me."

Yugi lifts his head to look at me. I think he is surprised by the calm tone of my voice.

"Now I want to show you something," I say.

CHAPTER 19

SEEING THE SUN LAND

One of our old stories tells about a journey that was
made by a group of seven young men.

This group of young men were friends. They
decided to find the place where the Sun rose, and
so they journeyed together to the east. They went
through strange lands and saw all sorts of people.

Finally they came to the edge of the world. There
they could see that the sky was a great arch of stone.
When that stone arch lifted up at dawn, the sun
passed through the doorway that was opened.
One of those young men tried to pass through that
doorway to see the land that Sun came from. But the
sky arch came down and crushed him.

Sadly, his six friends turned around and began the

long journey back to their homeland. It took so long
that they were all old men when they got there.

That story is on my mind as I sit with my friend
Yugi. Like that young man who lost his life, I have
six friends. Or I used to before they became afraid of
my father and me. But am I also like that one young
man in another way? Am I attempting something as
foolish as trying to enter the land of the Sun? I hope
not. I do hope that the journey I've decided to take
will bring a new light to all our people and not end
in disaster.

But I can't take that journey alone. I need to be able to
convince at least one person that what I am doing is not
witchcraft. What I am doing is for the good of our people.

Yugi is waiting to see what I will show him. I can
see that he is worried. Part of him is wondering if I
will do something bad, if I will try to work bad medicine on him. Yet part of him also sees me as his friend
and wants to trust me. His two hands are clenched together. Soon he will start rubbing them in that nervous
way of his.

Of all my friends, Yugi has always been the closest.
He is the only one of my friends who's cared enough
about me and had courage enough to seek me out and

warn me. He's always been the best listener of all of us. Still, I can see that he is uncertain. I have to be careful in what I say. But I do have an idea. I take a deep breath.

"My friend," I say, "can I ask you a question?"

Yugi looks confused, but he nods his head.

"Do we Tsalagi like horses?"

Yugi can't help but smile at that question. He loves horses. One of his goals in life is to join our Tsalagi Nation Lighthorse Police.

"Of course," he says.

"Did we always own horses?"

"No, the white men owned them first."

"That is true. And I have heard it said that when our people saw horses for the first time they ran away from them because those horses frightened them. People thought those horses were dangerous monsters."

Yugi nods. "I've heard that, too."

"Here is another question. Do we Tsalagi like guns?'

My friend nods again. "Of course we do, we . . ." Yugi pauses and lifts a finger to his mouth. He has always been a quick thinker. "But those guns were also first owned by the white men."

"And . . .?" I say.

"And when we first saw guns and heard them being

fired, we thought it was thunder and that those new weapons were magic."

"Good," I say. "Now let me ask you this question. Have we been told that the talking leaves belong only to the white men?"

Yugi pauses this time before he replies. But in the end he nods his head. "Yes," he says, more slowly but still in agreement.

I hold up my fist and then unfold my little finger. "The horse," I say. I unfold the next finger. "The gun." I unfold the third finger. "The book."

"Ah," Yugi says. "But we are getting the book now. We are being taught how to read and write English."

"Yes," I agree. "But is that the best way for us to use those talking leaves? My father does not think so. He thinks we should make talking leaves of our own without having to use any English at all."

I take out the piece of charcoal I took from our fireplace and put into my pocket. "Look." With it I begin to draw shapes on top of that flat stone.

"This," I say, "is how my father kept track of the things bought from him on credit at his store. Such as wagon wheels and cheeses." I draw the larger and smaller circles that stand for those things.

"I can see that," my friend says.

"Now here," I say, "is how he remembered the name of each person." I try to draw a small picture of two animals. My drawing is not very good, but I hope Yugi can see what I intend.

"What are these?" I ask.

"Two squirrels," Yugi replies after studying them for a while. "Ah, so that would mean someone named Two Squirrels."

"Yes. And who would this be?" I ask as I draw a nail.

"Yugi," he says, smiling for the first time as he does so. "Nail. That would be me."

"So," I say, "you see how pictures can speak. And that was my father's first idea. He would make a picture for every word. Then people could just look at those pictures and read the message."

Yugi strokes his chin. "That makes sense," he says. "But how many pictures would you have to draw?"

"Too many," I say. "My father tried to do just that. It took him years. He is very stubborn."

Yugi chuckles. "I know someone else like that."

I am not sure what he means, but I press on, pleased that his confusion has turned to amusement.

"That was what he was doing all those years in his little cabin, drawing pictures of our Tsalagi words. He did that until his neighbors became frightened—just like now—thinking he was doing sorcery. That was when they burned his cabin and all of the word pictures he had drawn."

"Ah," Yugi says, rubbing his hands together. He's still in agreement with me, but even this brief mention of witchcraft and the way our people respond to it is making him nervous.

"But then my father got another idea. He saw how the *Aniyonega* used little signs to make their words."

I pause, then sing, "*A, B, C, D* . . ."

Yugi nods. After all, he too has been taking those lessons in English at the missionary's cabin. Except he has continued and gone further than me.

"*E, F, G,*" he sings back to me. "The alphabet."

"That is right," I say. "But instead of using letters to spell words, my father got another idea. His idea was to use alphabet letters and new designs he invented to stand for Tsalagi sounds."

"Sounds?" Yugi says. There is confusion on his face again. But I am no longer worried. He has come this far with me. He is not going to turn and run away.

"Look at this," I say.

I have not yet mastered all of the signs for my father's way of writing, but I know enough of them now to be able to do what needs to be done next.

I use the charcoal to draw the sign for *Yu*. Ᏻ.

"Ᏻ," I say.

Then I draw the next syllable. "Ᏹ." *Gi*.

"Aha!" Yugi says. "My name?"

"Yes!"

I draw three more of my father's designs below the two that have spoken my friend's name. "And here is how we write the name of our people. *Tsalagi*."

Ꮳ

Ꮃ

Ᏹ

Yugi studies the symbols. A look has come over his face. It is like that of someone seeing the full light of dawn for the first time. His two hands let go of each other. He reaches out one finger to touch the signs for his own name. Then he touches the signs written in charcoal below it.

"Ᏻ . . . Ᏹ?" he reads aloud. Then "Ꮳ . . . Ꮃ . . . Ᏹ?"

He looks up at me. "Is it that easy?"

"Yes," I say. "It is that easy to read our language once you learn those symbols."

My friend has grasped some of what I have just shown him. But I can sense that he is not yet convinced of its importance—aside from the fact that he no longer worries that my father's work is witchcraft. However, I can understand why he has not yet realized what my father's creation means. It was not easy for me to realize just how vital having our own talking leaves could be.

"Do you remember what the missionary has often told us? How reading and writing is a useful thing?" I ask.

"It is," Yugi agrees. "You can send messages far away, keep records of important things so that they will be remembered. Reading and writing can be used to bring people together. Our missionary has even told us that the reason the English and the Americans became so powerful is because they have reading and writing."

"Could being able to read and write help our people then?"

"Of course," Yugi says. "That is why my parents have encouraged me to go to the missionary's school. My father has said that if we Tsalagi are able to read and write we may gain power like the white men." He pauses. "But why would we need to read and write in Tsalagi? Things can already be written in English."

"How many of our people can speak English as well as a white person?" I ask him.

"Very few," he says, shaking his head. "It is a hard language to learn. It does not make sense the way Tsalagi does."

"Do most of our people want to learn English?"

Yugi shakes his head again. "Most of our people do not trust writing in the English language. They say it is just used to deceive us. When we make agreements with the white men and they write them down, the things they write are seldom what we agreed to."

"But if our people could use our own language in our own way, read and write in Tsalagi, might they want to learn then?"

Yugi strokes his chin. "Uh-huh," he says. "They might. They might, indeed!"

He slaps his hands together so suddenly that it startles me. "Yes," he says. "Yes!"

If the light I saw in his eyes before was like the first rays of dawn, what is shining from his face now is as bright as noon on a cloudless summer day!

Yugi takes me by the arm. "My friend," he says. "I am sorry I doubted you. How can I help?"

❖❖❖ CHAPTER 20 ❖❖❖

LEARNING

The sun is in my heart now. My friend no longer doubts me and may even be my ally. I have won one small victory. I am smiling as I watch him walk away. He turns once to touch his chest and then waves at me.

Yes.

But this has been only the first battle I have to fight. I know that what comes next will not be easy. The next thing I have to do is convince my mother.

The white men do not understand just how important women are among the Tsalagi. In their world, women seem to have little power. Their main jobs are to take care of the homes and raise the children. They make none of the important decisions and they seem to own nothing—not even themselves.

It is very different among our people. One of our oldest stories tells of First Man and First Woman.

They lived together happily. But then one day, First Man did something that upset First Woman.

"You have hurt my feelings. I will live with you no longer," First Woman said. Then she turned her face to the east and walked away.

First Man was immediately sorry. But he could not stop her. He followed her to apologize, but he could not catch up to her. So he looked around for help. He looked up to the sky to *Une'lahun'ne*, the Sun, who is the oldest and wisest of all the women.

"Great One," First Man said to the Sun, "help me."

Sun saw that First Man truly was sorry and so she decided to help him. She shone down on the earth in front of First Woman to make huckleberries grow in her path. But First Woman did not stop. The Sun made blackberries grow and serviceberries, but First Woman just kept walking. It was not until Sun made strawberries, which spread across the ground in front of her, that First Woman paused. Those berries smelled sweet and each was the shape of a heart. As soon as First Woman tasted them, she remembered her husband and she could go no farther. She turned her face back to the west. She began to gather some of those berries to share with him.

So it was that First Man was finally able to catch up to her.

"I am sorry," he said.

"Have some of these," First Woman replied.

So it is that ever since then the first berries to ripen every year are the strawberries. And when we pick them, they remind us of the importance of being kind to one another . . . and of the strength of women.

Among our people, it is the women who are the heads of our households. They are the owners of the house. Every child belongs to his or her mother's clan. When a man marries, he goes to live in his wife's house among the people of her clan. If her husband does not behave properly, a woman can end their marriage. Then her husband must leave her house and go home to his mother. That is why my father had to leave when his marriage to my mother was ended.

In so many ways, our women have always been at the head of our people. None of our leaders could ever take office without the approval of the women. It is true that some things have changed since the coming of the *Aniyonega*. The Beloved Woman no longer sits in council next to the chief, but the power of our women is still great.

So, now that Yugi has gone back to his mother's house, it is to my own mother that I must go. As I walk along I am putting together my words, gathering them one by one. By the time my mother's cabin comes in sight, I am certain of what I have to say. But as soon as I walk through the door and my mother looks at me— in that way of hers which suggests that she is reading my mind—I cannot remember even one of the fine words I have been stringing together like the shells in a necklace.

"Ah," I say, "ah . . ."

My mother turns her head sideways to study me. I feel ever more uncertain. Then she smiles. "Sit, my son. You look hungry."

I had not realized it, but like almost everything my mother says, her words are true. As soon as I sit down at her table, my mouth is watering and my spoon is in my hand. I eat the corn bread and the rabbit stew that she places in front of me as if I was starving. Food is such a great gift from the Creator that when one eats, that food is all that one should think about. And so it is with me. Eating my mother's good food is the only thing in my thoughts until I pick up the last golden crumb from my plate and run my finger along the edge of the bowl for the last drop of stew.

But now that I have finished eating, now that my bowl is empty and I am sitting across from my mother, now I have to turn my thoughts back to the reason I just came back home.

I look over at her. Her face is calm. I'm not sure that mine is.

"Mother," I say . . . and that is as much as I can manage to say. I swallow and try again. "Mother . . ." I hold my breath.

"Yes, Uwohali," my mother says, "that is who I am." Then she smiles and that smile of hers is so reassuring and says so much that I am able to breathe again and relax.

"Do you know what I want to talk to you about?" I ask her.

In reply she reaches down into her lap and lifts up a piece of paper, a very familiar piece of paper that she places on the table between us. It is the sheet on which I have been practicing my father's designs. I should have known that there was no place in her house that I could hide anything from my mother. I bite my lip, but the smile has not disappeared from her face. She doesn't seem to be upset or afraid of those markings that struck such terror into the hearts of some of our people that they have been speaking even louder about . . . doing something.

"My son," she says, "your father was not a good husband, but that was not because I feared him or the things he did. Even when he was drunk, he never lost his gentle nature. Our marriage could not last because he cared so much about other things that there seemed to be no space in his life for his family. Now it seems he is a better father than he was back then. I have heard how devoted he is to your half sister. And if he has shared these . . . markings . . . with you, I do not believe that he intends any harm. I believe he is trying to be a father to you as well."

I nod my head. My eyes are moist. "That is what I believe, too," I say, my voice a little choked as I do so.

"Osdadu," my mother says. "Good." She taps her finger on the paper that lies on the table between us but has not come between us. "Now tell me about these markings."

"Gahgayyouee, Etsi!" I say. "I love you, mother." And then, like a stream that was dammed and has finally

broken through, my words spill out so fast I can hardly stop talking. I share with her my father's belief in the importance of writing and reading our own language. I explain how each design stands for a sound in our language just like the English alphabet. How my little sister, Ahyokah, is helping my father. How I have become determined to help him, too. I tell her how I have managed to convince my friend Yugi that it is not witchcraft. But there are still so many of our people who do not understand, who think my father, Sequoyah, is insane or doing evil magic.

And that is why I have come to her.

"Nothing good," I say, "can ever be done among our people if our mothers do not understand and help us," I say.

I've probably said too much. For one, my mother, intelligent as she is, has never been interested in reading and writing English.

"All those sounds in English are so strange," she has said in the past. "I can speak some of their words, but those scratches like little insects on their talking leaves look too hard to learn for an old woman like me."

So my comparing my father's writing to the English alphabet probably meant nothing to her. But the look on my mother's face is not one of confusion.

There is agreement in her eyes that I should try to follow my father's path. She believes—because I believe it—that his work can bring good to our Tsalagi people! And there is also this other look on her face that I know very well. She is looking up at the ceiling—not to see what is up there, but because she is making a plan.

I wait while she is thinking. Then she shakes her head.

"It will not be easy," my mother says. "There are people whose minds are so hardened against your father that it will take much work to get them to change. There are even some who want to take matters into their own hands."

My mother grasps my shoulders with her strong hands. "So you must be careful where you go now. Do not go into those sections of our town where those who are whispering about witchcraft live. Avoid the trails where someone might lie in wait. I cannot tell your father this. He believes that his good intentions will protect him. But you, my stubborn son, you must be wiser to protect yourself—and perhaps your innocent father, as well. So, if you are now going to follow your father's path, you must promise me that you will take care."

"I promise," I say, a lump in my throat as I say it. But I say it with certainty. My mother's words have both made me more aware of the dangers of helping my father and more certain that this is the work I must do.

My mother sighs. *"Hawa,"* she says. "Okay." She presses her lips together. "Now," she says, "you say that your friend Yugi understands this work and wants to help you."

"Yes, but his father has told him to stay away from me."

"Women's work," my mother says. "That is what is needed now." She stands up and dusts off her apron. It's what she always does after she has been cooking. Of course there is no flour on that apron right now that needs to be cleaned off. But I understand. She is not thinking of flour, but the foolish thoughts that need to be cleared away from the minds of our people.

"Come along," she says. "We are going to the house of Nancy Youngbird."

Nancy Youngbird is Yugi's mother. My mother and Yugi's mother are cousins and belong to the same clan—as do Yugi and I, of course. But Yugi's mother is several years younger. As a result she has always looked up to my mother as a wiser older sister.

My mother is a very forceful person. Now that I

think of it, I suppose some of my own stubbornness also comes from her. Once her mind is made up, it might as well be carved into stone.

Yugi and I are on the ground in front of his mother's cabin. We've drawn a circle in the dirt and are supposedly playing marbles. But neither of us is paying much attention to our shots. We are listening to the conversation our mothers have been having on the front porch as they sit together working on a quilt. My mother has explained what my father has been doing even better than I explained it to her. They've looked over at us once or twice during the conversation. And out of the corners of our eyes we've seen that the expression on their faces were those every son likes to see— protective, approving, perhaps a little surprised at how grown up their little boys have become.

"So, you will talk to your husband?" my mother finally asks, snipping a thread as she did so. The way she says that is not really a question.

"It would be good for me to talk to him," Yugi's mother replies. "Could you hand me that patch?"

My mother does so and for a time there is no sound but the smooth hissing of needles and thread through cloth.

"So," my mother asks, "we are in agreement?"

And as Yugi's mother sews on a patch of the quilt, which depicts a rising sun, she firmly nods her head. "We are in agreement, my older sister," she says.

My mother stands up and dusts off her apron.

"Osdadu," she says. And then my mother and I leave.

It is the next day. Yugi is telling me about what happened when his father came home.

"I was eager to hear what my mother would say to my father," Yugi says. "But that was not to be. As soon as my father walked in, my mother turned to me.

"'My son,' she said. 'I need you to run an errand for me. Go now!'"

Yugi shakes his head in amusement. "So I went, leaving my mother alone with my father—who already looked confused about what was going on. I walked down to the river, tossed a few rocks into the water, and then tried drawing some of your father's symbols in the mud. Finally, when I thought I had been gone long enough, I went back home. My mother was in the kitchen sweeping up the pieces of several dishes that had somehow been broken. There was a little smile on her face that she tried to hide by turning away as I came into the cabin.

"'Your father,' she said, 'is out on the back porch and wishes to speak with you.'

"It was hard for me not to laugh. My father always likes to pretend that he is the one who runs our household. 'My son,' he said. 'I, ah . . . ah . . .'"

Yugi chuckles. "My father paused just then because he looked up and saw that my mother was standing in the doorway watching us. 'I, er, we have decided,' my father said. 'Is that not so, my wife? Yes, we, your mother and I, have decided that it is good for you to learn this thing. Is that not so, my wife? Yes, that is what I have decided.'"

❖❖❖ CHAPTER 21 ❖❖❖

FOOTSTEPS

The night is darker than I'd expected. The full moon should have been lighting my way, but clouds must have blown in to cover the sky while Yugi and I were working together on learning my father's syllabary.

As soon as he looked out of the door of his mother's cabin and saw just how dark it was, Yugi turned to me.

"Uwohali," he said, "my friend, it is later than we thought. You must spend the night here."

"No," I said. "It will be fine. I have walked the trail between your house and mine so many times that I could do so with my eyes closed. My mother is expecting me and will worry if I do not come home."

So, despite his misgivings, I set out on my way.

At first, the walk seemed easy. Perhaps it was because we had made so much progress in our learning that I felt so sure of myself. And this was, indeed, a walk I'd made countless times before. But this night was unusually dark. So dark that I stumbled over a stone in the road and fell to my hands and knees. And that is when all of my certainty left me.

For in that moment before I began to rise to my feet again, I heard a sound behind me. It was a sound that sent a shiver down my back, a sound I recognized as footsteps. Only a few steps before whoever it was that followed me stopped. And the fact that those footsteps stopped worried me even more than hearing the sound of those feet following me.

I realize now how foolish I've been. I should have stayed at Yugi's cabin. The silence behind me means that whoever it is, is trying to be unheard, matching their steps to mine. And what is even worse is that I am certain what I heard was not the sound of only one person walking, but at least two.

Even on the darkest night, the sky is always a bit brighter than the land. So I do something my uncle Red Bird taught me. I do not rise to my feet, instead, I put my head as close to the ground as possible and look back along the road. And, just as he taught me, I am able to see something. There, outlined against the sky, are the shapes of two people, no more than a stone's throw behind me, both standing still and keeping quiet.

Who could it be? All I can see are their outlines, but from the size of them, they look to be grown men. And though I do not know who they are, I think I can guess. They are two of those men Yugi heard speaking at the store about burning Sally Guess's cabin and killing my father and my sister and me. Udagehi's father, perhaps, and one other. And I do not think I have to guess why they are following me. They mean to do me harm.

What shall I do now? If I leap up and try to run, that will alert those men that I am aware of them. They will start running, too. Maybe they have torches with them that they will then light. And because I'll be running without light, I might just trip and fall again or run into something. Then they will surely catch me.

Never show danger that you are afraid of it. Those were Red Bird's words. I speak them to myself in my mind as I stand up.

Never show danger that you are afraid of it.

Then, pretending to be unaware of the men following me, I rise to my feet and begin to walk.

As I walk, the wind changes. It's no longer blowing in my face, but coming from behind me, from the direction of those men stalking me. It brings to me a faint scent that I recognize all too well, the same smell that was on my father's breath in those days when I was a small child and he was almost always drunk. Alcohol! The men following me have been drinking. And that worries me even more, for a drunk man will do awful things that he would not do when sober.

I keep walking, hoping my pace is just quick enough to stay ahead of those following me. But what if they are not the only ones? What if other men are waiting ahead of me, waiting in ambush?

I look up at the sky. Is it brighter than it was before? Yes. That same wind at my back is also blowing high above me. It is moving the clouds away from the face of the moon. Now there's only a thin layer like tattered lace across the sky. And now the moon is beginning to show and her light is being cast on the land, making the path before me clearly visible.

I risk a quick glance over my shoulder. And I am both glad that I did so and frightened at the same time. Those two men have come closer. They're no more than a hundred feet behind me. I still can't make out their faces, but I can see that both of them are carrying heavy clubs.

"Stop!" one of them shouts, his voice slurred from drinking.

"Do not move!" the other man yells, raising one of his arms. "Stay there."

That is a command that I would be foolish to obey. There's only one thing for me to do now.

Run!

Flight is my best hope right now. Just then something whizzes past my face as I take to my heels, moonlight flashing off it as it just misses me.

A knife was just thrown at me, I think, and run even faster.

I hear their feet pounding the earth behind me, but I don't look back.

"Stop," the first man shouts again.

The men behind me are larger than me, armed with clubs and perhaps even more knives. Drunk as they are, they will not hesitate to do the worst to me if they catch me. But because they are drunk, perhaps they will not be able to run as swiftly or as sure as they could when sober. And though I am not the fastest runner among the boys of my age, I am far from being the slowest.

My attackers are no longer shouting. They are just concentrating on trying to catch me. But I can tell from the sounds of their heavy breathing and their feet thudding against the trail, that I am gaining ground. They

204

are farther behind me. The moonlight is so bright now that it casts shadows on the trail.

But my mother's cabin is still some distance away. The moon is bright now, but the clouds are still moving across the sky and its light may be blotted out again soon, well before I reach the safety of my home. And there are narrow places on the trail ahead of me where someone might be waiting in ambush. There is a prickling at the back of my neck, another sense beyond sight or smell or hearing that is warning me of more danger than those two pursuers who are now so far behind they have lost sight of me.

Where?

I slow my pace just enough to scan the trail ahead of me. There! That has to be the spot, there where a huge old oak tree overhangs the main path. If I keep going, I'll reach that narrower place in the path before the clouds blot out the moon again. I don't see any motion there, but I can sense a presence. Someone, another attacker, is waiting there to waylay me.

I can't go on and I can't turn back. But luck is with me because I have come to the one place along this trail that circles around Willstown where I have a chance of escape. The steep ravine that falls off to my left is the one that holds the hidden path to the Four

Bears. I find its entrance just as the moon again begins to slip into its cloak of clouds.

I duck down, push a branch aside to enter the nearly vertical hidden trail, slide down it perhaps fifty feet. Then I stop, holding on to the base of a sapling to keep myself from slipping. If I go any farther the sounds of brush rustling and stones dislodged by my feet rattling down the hill may give me away.

Just in time. I hear heavy feet—coming not from one direction on the trail but two. Then there is the scratching sound of flint striking steel, a spark, and then light as torches are set flaming. I can barely see the light through the heavy brush above me, but even so I close my eyes and lower my head so that no stray beam of light will reflect from my face.

"Did . . . you see . . . the boy?" Though his voice is still slurred by drink and he is breathing hard, I recognize who is speaking. It's Udagehi's father.

"We . . . we . . . were right behind him," a second voice speaks, the voice of the man who raised his hand and threw that knife at me.

"No," says a third voice, that of the man I sensed waiting in ambush. "I saw nothing. Are you sure he went this way?"

I listen as they continue to talk, stumbling about

as they do so. I keep my head down, trusting that they will not find the hidden entrance to my secret trail.

Then there's another sound.

Whoot-too-whoo.

The call of an owl from the branches of one of the trees next to the trail. Although another thought comes to me as I hear that call. Is it really an owl? Or is it my father, who can make any sound like that of the king-fisher when he came upon me at the stream?

"Eeee-yah!" one of the men cries, fear in his voice. "Did you hear that?"

That first owl's call is answered by another from deeper in the woods.

Whoot-too-whoo.

"Ah-ah-ah!" Udagehi's father says. "Two of them!"

Among our Tsalagi people, the owl is usually seen as a bird of ill omen. Some say that sorcerers can take the shape of an owl, and it is believed that the call of an owl can mean someone is about to die.

But I also know that it is not at all unusual to hear owls hoot like that at this time of year. It's the time of year when the owls call to one another this way, hoping to find a mate. I learned that from my uncle Red Bird, who told me that sometimes an owl is just an owl and that people who are feeling guilty will always find something to fear.

Like those three men on the trail above me. Those men do not like the sound of those owls. And whether it is really an owl or my father protecting me, the result is the same.

"Forget the boy."

"This is an evil night."

"Let us leave here now!"

Their frightened voices and heavy footsteps grow fainter as they move away.

Perhaps it would be safe for me to come out and continue home. But perhaps not. I make my way down the steep trail until I come to the place where I can crawl through the bushes to the Four Bears. I lean against the nearest of the bears, feeling its comforting presence. Even though I have no blanket, the night is not cold and I close my eyes, certain the old stones will guard me.

The next thing I know, a hand is grasping my shoulder, shaking me.

"Uwohali, Uwohali?"

I open my eyes. The bright daylight filtering in through the trees that arch overhead blind me for a moment. Where am I? Then I remember. I am at the

Four Bears. The one who just pulled me out of sleep must have been my friend Yugi. Who else knows this secret place?

But to my great surprise, as my eyes focus, I see that it is not Yugi at all. It is a grown man, a large man with a wide face and dark eyebrows that join in the middle. I blink my eyes twice before I recognize him. It is my uncle White Raven.

"Are you badly hurt?" White Raven asks me in his deep voice, squinting at me as he speaks, his broad face showing a look of concern.

His words confuse me.

"What? No? Why do you ask that?"

Then I feel the stiffness on the right side of my face. I lift my hand to my cheek and it is painful to the touch. Something dry is stuck to my face all the way down to my neck. Blood. The knife that was thrown at me didn't miss me after all. It must have been so sharp that when it grazed my cheek I didn't feel it cut me.

"Hold still."

My uncle keeps his left hand on my shoulder as he explores the side of my face gently. Then he settles back on his heels.

"Just a small cut," he says. "I thought it might be something worse. But it bled so freely that your whole face on this side is caked with blood. Did you catch it on a sharp twig? And why did you spend the night here? Your mother was worried and came to my house to ask me to help find you."

"How did you find me here?" I ask.

White Raven chuckles. "Who told you about this place to begin with? Your mother, yes? And who do you suppose showed your mother how to find our Four Bears but her older brothers? Now, what happened?"

There's no point in keeping it from him. I tell him everything—about the men who pursued me, the knife that was thrown, the third person waiting in ambush, and how I recognized the voice of Sharp Teeth, Udage-hi's father. A look comes over my big uncle's face like a dark cloud. White Raven has always been known to be peaceful, but he is also very large and strong. I have heard it said that no one ever wants to face his anger—like the anger that is darkening his eyes right now. I worry for a moment if he is thinking about taking revenge on Sharp Teeth. Then another look comes over White Raven's face as his thoughts take him in another direction. I remember how this uncle of mine has also become known for his political skills, for working with people rather than opposing them.

He reaches out a hand to pull me to my feet.

"Come along, nephew," he says, determination in his voice. "First we take you home to your mother. Then, when my brother returns from his travels, we will speak with your father and our village chief. It is time we found a way to put an end to this foolishness."

CHAPTER 22

THE VILLAGE CHIEF'S VISIT

Several more days have passed. Each day both Yugi and I have gone to work with my father at his wife's cabin—being careful to always stay on the main road and avoiding any of the small trails where someone might lie in wait. Am I afraid? No, I am not afraid. I am like my father. I am becoming a man and so I am not afraid. Instead, I am determined.

It's a bright morning. A sun as golden as the one on the quilt our mothers made is shining in through the window. As Yugi and I sit at the table, practicing our writing under my father's gentle guidance—and with the help of my somewhat annoying but bright little sister, Ahyokah—a voice calls from outside.

"*Oginawlee*, my friend," the voice calls. "Are you home? It is me, Agili."

Agili is our village chief.

My father stands and limps over to open the door, a smile on his face. "Welcome," he says. "*Wado*. Thank you for coming. Come in."

It is not a surprise that Agili has arrived. I am the one who was sent yesterday to invite him to come to see my father because there was something important that Sequoyah wished to share.

Agili had listened to my invitation, a serious look on his face. Then, just as my father had said he would do, he had run his finger along his nose three times and nodded.

"Tell my cousin," Agili had said, "that I will meet him tomorrow morning at his wife's house."

And now he has come as he promised. My father steps aside but Agili does not enter. He remains just outside the door. He is a tall, distinguished man, with a long face and a high forehead. He has a reputation for his great intelligence and his honest and forthright ways. Like my father, he served in the Red Stick War, but he did so as a major, a leader of many men. He also is a fluent speaker of English, which is another reason for his position as the head of our village. Dealing with the *Aniyonega* and helping protect us from the desires of some of them to cheat us and to take even more of our land is another of his jobs. The white men know him as George Lowrey, which was also the name of his white father. However, Agili, He Is Rising, is his true Tsalagi name.

His ears, like many of the men of his generation have lobes that have been cut and stretched so that they hang down almost to his shoulders. He is wearing large, round silver earrings as big as the palm of my hand and a nose ring the size of a silver dollar. Those were made several years ago by my father. His wearing them today is, I think, both a sign that he still respects and sees him as a friend.

"How are things with you, cousin?" Agili asks. His words are polite, but he is still staying on the porch.

My father smiles and nods, rubbing his chin with two fingers as he does so. "They are well," he says. "And getting better."

Agili shakes his head. "That is not what I am hearing. Before, people were just whispering about you. Now some of the more foolish ones are saying these things out loud. I have spoken and told them just how foolish they are. But I cannot tell another person what to think. And when someone's ears are closed to reason, it is hard to convince them that their thoughts are wrong. I am worried for your safety." Agili looks in at me. "And the safety of your family."

Sequoyah just nods, the gentle smile still on his face. "Come in," he says again. "I will show you something."

Agili is still hesitant. He slowly lifts one foot, like one about to wade into dark water without knowing how deep it is. He lifts his hand to run his finger along his nose. Once, twice, three times. Then he steps over the threshold.

"Osdadu," my father says. "Good. Now let me show you something."

He limps over to the table where we are sitting. Agili follows close behind him.

My father nods toward Yugi and me. "They are learning to write," he says. "They are just beginning to learn. Soon they will be able to do as I do. I can write down anything that any of our people can say. Anything. Then I can put it aside and pick it up later and there find all of it just as it was said."

He picks up a folded piece of paper and opens it. "This is a message that I took down over a month ago in Arkansas from Chief John Jolly. At first, like you and most of our people here, he was uncertain about what I made. But when I showed him how it worked, how it could help our people, he became convinced.

"So, asking me to use my way of writing, he spoke this message to bring to you. It says this:

215

*"'My cousin and clan brother Agili, this is
John Jolly sending you this message. I ask if you
are well. I urge you again to think of joining us
here in these new lands away from the Aniyonega. Now I send you my greetings in this
new way that Sequoyah has made. Now we
can have our own talking leaves just as do the
Aniyonega. I will now tell you something so
that you know this message is from me and no
one else, I will remind you of something that
only you and I know about. Do you remember
when we were little boys and took that pie
from the window where it was cooling? Do you
remember how we took it into the woods and ate
it? Do you also remember how you were then
stung on the lip by a wasp that also wanted that
pie? Do you remember how sad I was that you
were stung because it meant I had to eat the rest
of that pie all by myself?'"*

Agili is smiling by the time my father finishes reading. "This is all true," he says. "I am sure you are bringing
me a message from my cousin."

He pauses then and the smile vanishes from his face

the way the sun disappears when a cloud crosses in front of it.

"But it may be," Agili says, a suspicious tone entering his voice, "that you are not reading as do the *Aniyonega*. It may be that you just are not forgetful. It may be that those marks on the paper just help you remember things the way the patterns on a wampum belt help us to remember things."

I bite my lip. So many thoughts are going through my mind now. What if, no matter what my father says or does, he is not able to convince Agili? Agili may be my father's cousin, but he is still the village chief. I do not think that Agili believes my father's work is black magic. At least I hope that is so. But what if Agili decides that my father's work is false and foolish, or that my father really is crazy or, worse, that Sequoyah is just trying to deceive him? What if he decides to banish my father from our village and sends him back to Arkansas? What will I do then?

But my father does not look worried at all. He had not expected to win a victory that easily.

"No," my father says, "I do not remember what I have written. And these marks stand for the sounds of our talking. Those marks make different words depending on where I place them."

Agili looks confused.

My father sees that confusion, but it still does not trouble him. "I have a better way to show you how this works." He looks back at us. "Ahyokah," he says.

My little sister shoots up from her seat on the other side of our table like a partridge bursting out of a tree when someone gets too close. She skips to my father's side, her eyes shining with excitement. She knows what she is about to be asked to do.

My father picks up the page on which the eighty-six marks of the syllabary are written. "Read this for your uncle," he says.

Ahyokah takes the page firmly in both of her small hands, straightens her back, takes a deep breath, and begins to read.

"A, Ga, Ka, Ha . . ."

She reads them rapidly, but speaks each sound clearly and well. When she reaches the end, my father pats her on the shoulder.

"Now read it one more time. But start at the bottom. Then your uncle may hear that it is just the same."

Ahyokah presses her lips together, nods, and recites the list of syllables yet again, starting at the end of the list.

"Yv, wv, tsv, tlv . . ."

Again, she speaks every one of the eighty-six marks without a mistake.

"Yah!" Agili says when she is done. There is surprise in his voice. "That is interesting, indeed. But what was she saying? I could not understand. Was it another language? That sounded like Muskogee."

Sequoyah shakes his head. "No, my cousin. It is our language. But it is not our words. It is our sounds. You just need to put them together. Now look."

My father writes out three of those signs on a blank page, carefully pointing to each one with the stem of his long pipe before he writes it.

"Read this," he says to Ahyokah.

"Ꮯ-Ꮃ-Ꭹ," she says without a moment's pause. *Tsalagi.*

"Ah," Agili says, nodding, "perhaps I see."

"Now," my father says, "I can take the last of those syllables"—he writes it on the paper—"and place this other one in front of it, then this one behind it."

"ᎤᎩᎵ," my little sister reads, smiling up at our village chief and grasping him by his hand. *Agili.*

The sunshine of a true smile, as bright as the dawning of a new day, has come now to Agili's face.

CHAPTER 23

GOOD OR BAD

Although most of our people have been quick to adopt the useful things brought to us by the *Aniyonega*, there have always been those who worry that new things may prove to be harmful. Something that seems to be good may turn out in the end to be bad.

Some of our oldest stories warn about such things. One such tale is the one about the two boys and the Ukten.

Long ago, it is said, two boys were out hunting in a valley when they found a little snake. Its pale, shiny skin was beautiful, but it was thin and weak. That snake spoke to them.

"Help me or I will die," it said. "Feed me."

It was so beautiful and so helpless that the boys

took pity on it. They brought it birds and mice. The snake ate those birds and mice.

"Thank you," it hissed. "I will always be your friend. Now go get me more food."

Those boys did as the snake said. Every day they returned to the valley and brought it more and more food. That snake got larger and larger. The mice and little birds were no longer enough. Now they brought it squirrels and rabbits. Soon that big snake began to grow horns on its head. It was turning into an Ukten. But the boys did not notice the hungry way the snake looked at them.

"I am your friend," it would hiss to them each day. "Now go get me more food."

Those boys did not know the huge snake that was now an Ukten was planning to eat them and all the people of their village when it had grown large enough. They kept feeding it. Now they were bringing it deer. They were spending all their time hunting just to feed it.

One day, though, they heard a strange rumbling sound coming from the valley where the great snake lived. When they got to that valley they saw that great snake was engaged in a fight. It was fighting with Thunder, that strong old man who lives in the sky and hurls down arrows of lightning.

The Ukten was coiled all around Thunder, but Thunder had grasped its head and so it could not defeat him.

"Help me," the Ukten hissed to the boys. "Shoot him or he will hurl down his arrows and kill you and all your people."

"Boys," Thunder said in his deep, rumbling voice, "Do not listen to him. He has been tricking you. He is evil and plans to devour you and all your people."

"No," the Ukten hissed. "I am your friend. He is the one who is evil. He will kill you."

"My grandsons," Thunder rumbled, "hear me. I am the one who is truly your friend. Now shoot him in the seventh spot on his body."

Those boys knew that Thunder's words were true. They saw that the Ukten had been using its magic to deceive them. They fired their arrows at the seventh spot on the Ukten's body and it fell away.

So it is that ever since then our Tsalagi people have been the friends of Thunder.

My father only wants to bring something good to our people. His words and his actions have always been kind and friendly. Still, those doubters think that his pleasant manner is just a disguise. It hides something dark and dangerous. Witchcraft!

That is why this test has been set up by our village chief. Agili now believes in my father's work. But Agili is wise enough to know that it will take something dramatic to change the minds of those who are so afraid of this new thing my father has made that they think is evil. So afraid that they have now begun to talk openly about killing Sequoyah and his family—just as those boys killed the Ukten long ago.

I look around the Council House. It seems as if everyone in Willstown is here. All of my former friends and their families are among them. I try to make eye contact with some of them. But they turn their faces away or look down as soon as I look their way. I bite my lip, wondering once again if this is the right thing for us to do now. So much is at stake today!

The Council House is so full that there is no room for everyone. There are as many outside as there are within its walls. And everyone's mood is one of expectation. The sound of people talking in hushed voices as they wait for the test that has been set for today is like the sound of a strong wind through a grove of pines. The feeling in the air is like that before a storm.

Agili has called this meeting today. Because he is not just the chief of our town, but a very respected elder, people answered his call. But not all came because of their respect for our village chief. Some have flocked here today for another darker, bloodier reason . . . like ravens to a kill. They are the ones who have muttered the most about my father's talking leaves being evil magic. They are here in the expectation that his evil may be exposed. Their hope is that he will either be exiled forever or sentenced to death. I have heard that some of them have sworn that if the council does not sentence him to die, then they will take care of that themselves. It has been whispered that, no matter what is shown or decided today, Sequoyah and his family will not live to see another sunrise.

I wish I could be more helpful. I have been studying hard for more than two weeks now. But I have not yet learned my father's way of writing our language well enough. It should not take that much longer for me to be able to write it and read it as well as he does. All it requires is for me to memorize, recognize, and be able to draw those eighty-six shapes. My friend Yugi has also made good progress, even though he has not learned as much as I now know. I now can read and write more than half of the syllables.

But half is not enough. To be able to write anything said in Tsalagi or to read anything written in the syllabary one must know it all. And I do not.

Aside from Sequoyah, there is only one person who perfectly knows all of our syllabary. That one is my little sister, Ahyokah.

I look over at her and she smiles at me. She is not nervous at all. She and my father are both sitting there, their faces as calm as the surface of a pond on a sunny, windless day.

But I am not calm. I am so nervous that I feel sick to my stomach. Of course, that may just be because I am so hungry right now. When I got up this morning I forgot to eat anything before coming here to the Council House. I cannot think of another time in my life when I have been so worried about anything that I have forgotten to eat. My stomach rumbles as I think of that. It rumbles so loud that, if there were not so many people talking, it would have been heard by everyone around me.

Someone nudges my side. I turn. It's Yugi.

To my surprise, he does not look worried at all. In fact, he looks quite confident. He trusts me more than I trust myself. I just hope I have not led him onto a path that will lead us over a cliff!

"Uwohali," he whispers, leaning close to my ear, "that sound of thunder scared me! I thought I was about to see lightning shooting out of your belly button!"

He chuckles at his own joke. Then he hands me something wrapped in a cloth. "Your mother told me to give this to you before you starve to death."

I unfold the cloth and find four biscuits, still warm. I lean forward in my seat and see my mother sitting not far from us next to Yugi's mother. I had not noticed her till now. My mother motions toward her mouth.

Eat.

I eat those warm biscuits. As I do so, some of the anxiety I was feeling leaves me. But not all of it. I still do not know for sure how things will end this day. Will it be good or will it be bad? Will people truly listen and understand? What my father has made is such a powerful tool. It can bring our nation together as nothing else has ever done before. For all of our sakes—not just my family and my trusting friend Yugi, but all of our Tsalagi people—I hope that it will.

CHAPTER 24

THE TEST

Agili stands in front of the crowd, holding up his hands for silence.

I hold my breath. Will they pay attention to him? Some of the feelings against my father are so strong. But then one face turns to him and another and another. Gradually the low talking subsides. Soon it is as quiet as a forest grove after the wind stops whispering through the leaves.

"My friends and my neighbors," Agili says, "it is good that you are here. I have called you to gather so that you all may see this with your own eyes and hear it with your own ears. That way the word of what happened here will not reach you as gossip. You will be able to judge for yourself the worth of what my cousin will show you."

"Witchcraft," says a cold voice from somewhere in the crowd. "I already know what that is!"

A chill goes down my back at those words. The low murmur of agreement that goes through part of the crowd makes me even more worried. But that murmur dies down as Agili raises both hands higher.

"My friends," he says, his voice louder and firmer than before, "you know it is not the way of our people to judge something until we know what we are judging. So let us wait. Let us watch and listen."

He looks around the crowd. No one else speaks.

"Good," he says. Then he turns toward my father and motions with his chin for him to move forward.

My father does so, with Ahyokah by his side.

"My friends," Sequoyah says, "you may believe that talking leaves belong only to the white people. That is no longer so. I have found a way so that we may record anything in our language using these marks."

He holds up a large piece of paper with the eighty-six signs of the syllabary drawn upon it.

"Bird footprints?" someone near the front says. I cannot see him, but I recognize the owl-like voice as that of Equgugu's father.

His words are answered by a little ripple of laughter from the people nearest him. But it is nervous laughter.

Though everyone has agreed to gather here, they are uncertain about what they are going to see. And I am uncertain about how they are going to respond.

My father remains calm, that small understanding smile on his face is not mocking or defensive.

"Yes," he says, "these do look a little like bird footprints. Your eyes are good, my friend. And we all know what bird footprints mean. They tell us where a bird has been, whether it was large or small, which way it walked before it flew on. But these marks mean much more than that."

He put his hand on Ahyokah's shoulder. "My daughter," he says, "she will help me show you what these marks mean." He points with his lips toward one of the trees on the far edge of the field next to the Council House. "Go."

Ahyokah runs past the front of the crowd, not stopping until she reaches that faraway tree.

"Now," my father says, "can my daughter hear what I am saying?"

"No." Several voices in the crowd answer as one.

"Good. Now," my father looks out at the crowd, "will someone speak a message to me?"

Big Rattling Gourd steps forward. I am relieved that he does so. He has long been a friend of my father's but has avoided seeing him since his return from Arkansas because of all the bad things being said. But after Agili's visit with my father, our town chief spoke to him. So two days ago, at Agili's suggesion, he came to my stepmother's cabin. Sequoyah showed him how he was able to make the leaves talk. It excited Big Rattling Gourd so much that he left saying that he would not be able to sleep that night.

"I will speak," Big Rattling Gourd says. "Record these words: Big Rattling Gourd just spoke. He asked if the talking leaves can really speak Tsalagi."

Sequoyah quickly writes the syllables. Then he hands the paper to Big Rattling Gourd, takes off his neckerchief, raises it high in the air, and waves it so that my sister can see his signal. As she begins to make her way back, my father speaks to the crowd.

"Now I will go over there."

By the time Ahyokah reaches us, my father is far away on the other side of the field. She holds out her hand and Big Rattling Gourd gives her the paper with the message on it. She climbs up onto a box that has been placed so that everyone in the crowd can hear her.

"THIS IS WHAT MY FATHER WROTE," Ahyokah shouts in a high clear voice, "'BIG RATTLING GOURD

JUST SPOKE. HE ASKED IF THE TALKING LEAVES CAN REALLY SPEAK TSALAGI.'"

A few people are turning and looking at one another in amazement. But everyone is not yet convinced. In fact, I see that some people are still muttering. My keen hearing is good enough to pick up what they are saying.

"That was easy," someone sneers. "*Tla!* It proves nothing."

"Just trickery," the woman next to him agrees.

"I still think it is witchcraft!" another person says.

My father is still far away on the other side of the ball field. My little sister is standing up there all by herself. Someone has to do something!

The next thing I know I have stood up and my legs are carrying me forward in front of the crowd. I stop when I am next to Ahyokah who looks up at me with trusting eyes and then reaches out to take my hand. Everyone is looking at us. But what should I do now? What can I say? Why did I put myself in front of the crowd like this?

I feel a hand on my shoulder. Someone else has joined us. It is my true friend Yugi.

"Go ahead," he says to me in a low voice. "You will know what to say."

I take one deep breath and then another. Then I speak in a voice so loud that it surprises even me.

"SPEAK ANY MESSAGE TO MY SISTER," I shout to the crowd. "SHE WILL WRITE IT AND MY FATHER WILL READ IT."

I hand my sister a piece of paper and the pen.

For a moment the crowd is silent. Then the person who just said that nothing had been proven stands up. I recognize him now as Black Fox, the father of my former friend Ugama. Ugama has remained sitting in the crowd and the look on his face is not unfriendly. In fact, he looks sad.

"I have a message to be written," Black Fox says.

He walks up and stands over my sister who has placed the paper on the table in front of her and is holding her pen.

"Write this," he says. Then he leans so close that even I cannot hear the words he whispers in her ear.

My sister calmly writes that message down. Then she hands Agili the paper. She turns to look at me, an impish grin on her face, and then runs off to stand by the same distant tree where she was before. And when my father comes back, he takes the paper and stands next to Black Fox, whose arms are defiantly crossed.

"I will read what is written," he says. The gentle smile on his face becomes a little broader. "Even though I do not agree with it." Then he reads the message my sister wrote.

"I, Black Fox, speak these words. We are not children who can be fooled by Sequoyah's tricks. His foolish marks cannot carry my words. If they do, then I, Black Fox, will eat the paper they are written upon."

Black Fox has uncrossed his arms and the look on his face has changed to one of amazement.

"You do not have to eat this paper, my friend," Sequoyah says. "Just tell me what you think now."

Black Fox turns to the crowd.

"Those are my words," Black Fox says. "I was wrong."

Some of people in the crowd are smiling now.

"It is true," I hear Equgugu's father say. "Sequoyah has found a way for the leaves to talk Tsalagi."

Not everyone is in agreement. I still hear a few cold voices of doubt in the crowd.

"All that has been proved," someone mutters, "is that both Sequoyah and his daughter are witches."

But before anything else can be said, Agili has placed

himself in front of us and is raising his hands again for silence.

"My friends," he says, "now you have seen and heard this. Some of you are convinced—as I am. But I know that some of you are still uncertain. You may see, as I see, the power of being able to read and write our own language.

"So I have an idea. Let us test Sequoyah's talking leaves further. Let us send word to our other towns and ask them to send us a few young men eager to learn. Let Sequoyah teach them how to use the talking leaves and then in every town have a public test until all of our people are of one mind. Shall we do this? I ask, SHALL WE DO THIS?"

"Uu!" Black Fox says. "Yes."

"Yes," says Yugi's mother from within the crowd.

Another says yes and then another. *Uu! Uu!* Yes! Yes! It washes through the crowd like a wind growing strength, like a wave moving the surface of wide water. Even those who still doubt can no longer be heard as the crowd begins to chant their agreement.

Yes, yes, let us do this.

And now I have no doubt. What we have begun will not end here. Instead, like a stone dropped into still waters, its ripples will spread far and wide. And when people see the power of my father's creation and begin to learn to use my father's syllabary, they will then teach others.

There is an old saying that the ice of winter never leaves all at once. It takes time for the thaw to happen. But when it does, nothing can stop the spring and summer from returning.

I stand between my father and my sister. My friend Yugi is close behind me with his hand on my shoulder. And I am smiling. I have found the path for my life. I no longer wonder what I can do, what I can make. I will help teach my people how to read and write our beautiful language. I will help bring our people closer together with Sequoyah's talking leaves. I will help our people stay strong, even in the face of the white men's might.

I will help bring our Tsalagi people that warmth of the sun.

AFTERWORD

Born somewhere between 1760 and 1780 in the Cherokee town of Tuskegee in present-day Tennessee, the Cherokee man known as Sequoyah was a true genius. In the words of one of his biographers, Grant Foreman, he was "the only man in history to conceive and perfect in its entirety an alphabet or a syllabary."

One of the amazing things about Sequoyah's invention is that it was so based in the actual sounds of their language that it was easy for Cherokee people to learn to read and write it. Within a few months, Cherokee people who had been totally illiterate were able to read and write using the syllabary. People of all ages were soon using the language to communicate with one another. When the Cherokee Nation began to publish its own newspaper, the *Cherokee Phoenix*, it was printed in both English and the Cherokee syllabary. It was a major unifying force and a source of great pride to all the Cherokees.

Sequoyah himself returned to Arkansas and eventually became one of the principal leaders of the western Cherokees. Beloved and respected by everyone, it was Sequoyah who worked to bring together the western Cherokees and their eastern relatives after the Trail of Tears when nearly all of the remaining Cherokees in the American South were forcibly removed to part of the Indian Territory that became Oklahoma. The Cherokee Trail of Tears took place in the winter of 1838–1839. By then Sequoyah himself was living in the West. However, during that terrible journey Sequoyah's son Tessee (or Jesse), on whom Uwohali, my main character in this novel is partially based, was one of the principal interpreters.

Sequoyah never stopped trying to bring his people together. In 1842, he heard that one band of Cherokee people had ended up in northern Mexico. He was determined to bring them back together with the rest of the nation. Even though he was not well, he made the long trip down through Texas accompanied by Tessee and six or seven other Cherokees. He died somewhere south of the Mexican town of San Cranto and was buried in an unmarked grave.

Sequoyah's life ended, but the legacy of his syllabary and the pride it inspired in his Cherokee people still lives on. Although English is today the primary language of the Cherokee Nation, Sequoyah's syllabary is still preserved and taught to each new generation. As long as there are Cherokee people, I have been told, Sequoyah's talking leaves will continue to speak.

SEQUOYAH'S

Cherokee Syllabary

Ꭰ a	Ꭱ e	Ꭲ i	Ꭳ o	Ꭴ u	Ꭵ v
Ꭶ ga Ꭷ ka	Ꭸ ge	Ꭹ gi	Ꭺ go	Ꭻ gu	Ꭼ gv
Ꭽ ha	Ꭾ he	Ꭿ hi	Ꮀ ho	Ꮁ hu	Ꮂ hv
Ꮃ la	Ꮄ le	Ꮅ li	Ꮆ lo	Ꮇ lu	Ꮈ lv
Ꮉ ma	Ꮊ me	Ꮋ mi	Ꮌ mo	Ꮍ mu	Ᏽ mv
Ꮎ na Ꮏ hna Ꮐ nah	Ꮑ ne	Ꮒ ni	Ꮓ no	Ꮔ nu	Ꮕ nv
Ꮖ qua	Ꮗ que	Ꮘ qui	Ꮙ quo	Ꮚ quu	Ꮛ quv
Ꮜ sa Ꮝ s	Ꮞ se	Ꮟ si	Ꮠ so	Ꮡ su	Ꮢ sv
Ꮣ da Ꮤ ta	Ꮥ de Ꮦ te	Ꮧ di Ꮨ ti	Ꮩ do	Ꮪ du	Ꮫ dv
Ꮬ dla Ꮭ tla	Ꮮ tle	Ꮯ tli	Ꮰ tlo	Ꮱ tlu	Ꮲ tlv
Ꮳ tsa	Ꮴ tse	Ꮵ tsi	Ꮶ tso	Ꮷ tsu	Ꮸ tsv
Ꮹ wa	Ꮺ we	Ꮻ wi	Ꮼ wo	Ꮽ wu	Ꮾ wv
Ꮿ ya	Ᏸ ye	Ᏹ yi	Ᏺ yo	Ᏻ yu	Ᏼ yv

CHEROKEE WORDS:

Ah-hey: an exclamation

Ani-tsa-guhi: the bears, Bear People

Ani-tsa-la-gi: real Cherokee

Ani-yonega: white people

Ani-yunwiya: "Principal People,"
the traditional Cherokee name for themselves

A-tsu-ta: my son

Awi Usdi: the little white deer,
the leader of the animals

Chunkey: game played with a rolled stone and poles

Echota: the Peace Town that was the former
capital of the Cherokee Nation

Edoda: father

Etsi: mother

Gah-gay-you-ee: I love you

Gi-li: dog

Ha-ha: no

Ha-wa: you're right, a word of agreement

Losi: Lucy

Madi: Maddie

Meli: Mary

O-gi-na-li: my friend

O-gi-naw-lee: Are you home?

O-s-da-du: it is okay, it is fine

Osgutan-uhi: pine tree

Osiyo and **Siyo :** hello

Sa-lo-li: squirrel

Sauh: snorting sound made by the deer

Taskigee (Also spelled Tahs-kee-gee) :
important Cherokee town on the Little Tennessee River
that was burned by the white people

Tla: dismissive exclamation

Tlah-huh: no

Tsa-la-gi: the name that became Cherokee,
probably from a Choctaw word meaning "cave dwellers"

Tsi-s-qua: bird

Tsi-yu: tulip poplar tree

Tsu-la: fox

Ukten: a water monster

U-le-la-nu-go: "Amazing Grace" (the hymn)

Une'-lahun'-ne: the sun

U-u (or v-v): yes

Wado: thank you

Wado agi etsi: thank you, my mother

Wa-heh: an exclamation

We-sa: cat

Ye-la-si-di: knife

FURTHER READING

"The Cherokees revere the memory of Sequoyah as the greatest Cherokee that ever lived. . . ." That is how Jack F. and Anna G. Kilpatrick expressed it in their collection of folktales of the Oklahoma Cherokee, *Friends of Thunder*.

The same may certainly be said about the general public as a whole—at least those who have any knowledge of this towering figure. In a way, he has become more myth than actual man. Because of the role he played, the amazing accomplishments of his life, a number of books, both nonfiction and fiction, have been written about him. Interestingly, though, both the fictional representations of his life and the imaginative recreations of his story often contain information that is speculative at best and historically inaccurate at worst. A truly authoritative, accurate, and comprehensive book about Sequoyah's life and accomplishments—not just as the creator of his syllabary but as a peacemaker and astute political leader—has yet to be written, and there are aspects of his life that will always remain a mystery.

The reading list that follows should not be seen as exhaustive or as a sole source of information. Consider it a starting point toward a deeper understanding of a people, a place, a history, and a time that I believe should be better known.

A Cherokee Encyclopedia by Robert J. Conley. University of New Mexico Press, 2007.

The Cherokee Nation: A History by Robert J. Conley. University of New Mexico Press, 2005.

History, Myths, and Sacred Formulas of the Cherokees (1890–1891) by James Mooney. Cherokee Publications, 2006.

Sequoyah by Grant Foreman. University of Oklahoma Press, 1938.

Sequoyah, the Cherokee Genius by Stan Hoig. Oklahoma Historical Society, 1995.

Sequoyah's Gift: A Portrait of the Cherokee Leader by Janet Klausner and Duane H. King. HarperCollins Publishers, 1993.

Trails of Tears, Paths of Beauty by Joseph Bruchac. National Geographic Society, 2000.

I also recommend visiting the websites of the Eastern Band of Cherokee in North Carolina, the Museum of the Cherokee (*www.cherokeemuseum.org/*), the Cherokee Nation of Oklahoma (*www.Cherokee.org*), and the Cherokee Heritage Center (*www.cherokee heritage.org/*)

ACKNOWLEDGMENTS

My interest in Cherokee history and culture stretches back more than five decades. This novel is the seventh book I've written or edited that focuses on the people who call themselves *Aniyunwiya*—the Principal People. *Aniyunwiya*, in fact, is the title of an anthology of contemporary writing by Cherokee authors that I edited two decades ago. Tsalagi, the name usually written as "Cherokee," seems to have been derived from "Cha-la-kee," a word in another southeastern indigenous language, Choctaw, that may be translated as "Those who live in the mountains." (It is amazing how many of the popular names used by non-natives are names those tribal nations never used to call themselves. Iroquois, Sioux, Navajo, Apache. The list is long.)

Although I have done extensive research using the written record, and I am including a brief reading list for those who wish to know more about the Cherokees, my deeper understanding of their rich and complex culture has come from Cherokee friends and teachers. I cannot stress enough how much their generosity has contributed and whatever is best in anything I have published that deals with this enduring, resilient nation has come from them. This current book, for example, owes a deep debt of gratitude to the people in the Cherokee language program at the Cherokee Nation in

Tahlequah, especially Roy Boney who reviewed the manuscript, made helpful suggestions, and made sure my use of their language and Sequoyah's syllabary was accurate.

The list of those Cherokee people who've taught me so much over the decades is too long for me to include everyone. So I will just mention some of those who most directly impacted this book. First is my friend, the late Robert Conley, the most prolific Cherokee author, who wrote a novel of his own about Sequoyah. Whenever we were together in Oklahoma or in North Carolina, or at some other gathering or conference outside the Cherokee nations, Bob was always offering me insights and introducing me to people who could take me further along the path of knowledge. And then there was his extremely Cherokee sense of humor, the way laughter and lessons were always combined whenever he was cracking a joke or engaging in gentle teasing. It's hard to express how much he is missed. As is another friend and teacher whose poetry was always informed by his Cherokee roots—the late Gogisgi/Carroll Arnett, who gave me my first insights in the Cherokee Nation from a Cherokee perspective over forty years ago.

Another longtime friend I must thank is Gayle Ross, surely one of the greatest storytellers in the world, much less among her own Cherokee people. Whenever I hear Gayle tell a traditional tale, a whole world opens up before me, and it has been my great fortune to now and then share the stage or engage in collaboration with her.

Chad Smith, the former Principal Chief of the Cherokee

Nation of Oklahoma, and Hastings Shade, the former Deputy Principal Chief—who never were too busy to talk with me whether over the phone or while I was visiting their nation.

There's Jerry Wolfe, storyteller, stickball maker, Beloved Man, and museum guide who told me the story of the great ball game between the birds and animals as we walked through the Cherokee Museum in Cherokee, North Carolina, and to whom I owe what I know about the game of chunkey.

There's Don Belt, an Oklahoma Cherokee who has been teaching the Cherokee language at the Cherokee Nation in North Carolina and provided a great deal of help when I was working on a project for National Geographic that became the book *Trails of Tears, Paths of Beauty*. There're Robert Bushyhead and Lloyd Arneach, Cherokee storytellers who were born and raised on the Qualla Boundary in North Carolina and who honored me by allowing me to write introductions for their books.

To those people and so many more Cherokees I say *Wado, wado*! I am thankful for their strength and their generosity. It is because of such people that the Cherokee Nations have, as Chad Smith put it, not just survived but thrived to the point where together they are today one of the most numerous of all the indigenous nations of the United States with close to 300,000 enrolled.

TURN THE PAGE FOR AN EXCERPT FROM
JOSEPH BRUCHAC'S CRITICALLY ACCLAIMED
NOVEL ABOUT THE NAVAJO MARINES
OF WORLD WAR II.

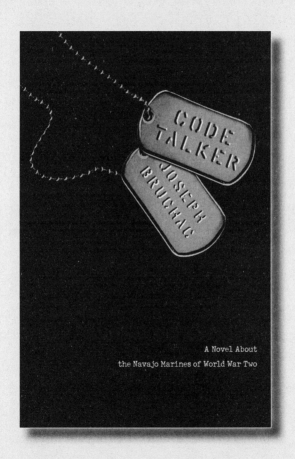

Listen, My Grandchildren

Grandchildren, you asked me about this medal of mine. There is much to be said about it. This small piece of metal holds a story that I was not allowed to speak for many winters. It is the true story of how Navajo Marines helped America win a great war. There is much that I must remember to speak for this medal, to tell its story as it should be told. I must remember not only the great secret with which I was trusted, but also all that happened to me and those like me. That is a lot. But I think that I can do it well enough. After all, I was expected to remember, as were the other men trained with me. The lives of many men depended entirely on our memories.

Look here. The man you see riding a horse on the back of this medal was an Indian. He is also one of those raising that flag there behind him. I knew him when we were both young men. His name was Ira Hayes. He was a fine person, even though he was not one of our people, but *Akimel O'odam*, a Pima Indian. We both fought on a distant island far off in the Pacific Ocean. There was smoke all around us from the exploding shells, the snapping sound of Japanese .25 caliber rifles, the thumping of mortars, and the rattling of machine guns. We could hear the pitiful cries of wounded men, our own Marines and the enemy soldiers, too.

It was a terrible battle. But our men were determined as they struggled up that little mountain. On top of it is where Ira was photographed, raising the flag of *Nihimá*. I was not one of those who fought to the top of Mount Suribachi, but I had my own special part to play. I helped send the message about our success, about the brave deeds so many Marines did that day for *Nihimá*.

Nihimá, "Our Mother." That is the Navajo word we chose to mean our country, this United States. It was a good name to use. When we Indians fought on those far-off islands, we always kept the thought in our minds that we were defending Our Mother, the sacred land that sustains us.

Nihimá is only one of the Navajo words we chose for places with *bilagáanaa* names. South America became *Sha-de-ah-Nihimá*, "Our Mother to the South." Alaska we called *Bee hai*, "With Winter." Because we knew that Britain is an island, we gave it the name of *Tó tah*, "Surrounded by Water." When we did not know much about a place, we described something about the people there. So we named Germany *Béésh bich'ahii*, "Iron Hat," and Japan was *Bináá'ádaálts'ozí*, "Slant-eyed."

Sometimes we didn't know much about either the country or the people there, but that did not stop us. We used our sense of humor and played with the English. The word we used for Spain was *Dibé diniih*, which means "Sheep Pain."

But I am getting ahead of myself. I have not even explained to you yet why we made up such names. I have not told you why being able to speak our Navajo language, the same Navajo language they tried to beat out of me when I was a child, was so important during World War Two. It was because I was a Navajo code talker.

What was a code talker and what did we code talkers do? Why was the secret we shared so great that we could not tell even our families about it until long after the war ended?

You cannot weave a rug before you set up the loom. So I will go back to the beginning, pound the posts in the ground, and build the frame. I will start where my own story of words and warriors begins.

CHAPTER ONE
Sent Away

I was only six years old and I was worried. I sat behind our hogan, leaning against its familiar walls and looking up toward the mesa. I hoped I would see an eagle, for that would be a good sign. I also hoped I would not hear anyone call my name, for that would be a sign of something else entirely. But the eagle did not appear. Instead, my mother's voice, not much louder than a whisper, broke the silence.

"Kii Yázhí, come. Your uncle is in the wagon."

The moment I dreaded had arrived. I stood and looked toward the hills. I could run up there and hide. But I did not do so, for I had always obeyed my mother—whose love for me was as certain as the firmness of the sacred earth beneath my moccasins. However, I did drag my feet as I came out from behind our hogan to see what I knew I would see. There stood my tall, beautiful mother. Her thick black hair was tied up into a bun. She was dressed in her finest clothing—a new, silky blue blouse and a blue pleated skirt decorated with bands of gold ribbons. On her feet were soft calf-high moccasins, and she wore all her silver and turquoise jewelry. Her squash-blossom necklace, her bracelets, her concha belt, her earrings—I knew she had adorned herself with all of these things for me. She wanted me to have this image of her to keep in my mind, to be with me when I was far from home.

However, the thing I saw most clearly was what she held in her arms. It was a small bundle of my clothes tied in a blanket. My heart sank. I really was going to be sent away.

My mother motioned toward the door of our hogan and I went inside. My great-grandfather was waiting for me on his bed. He was too weak to walk and was so old that he had shrunk in size. He had never been a big man, but now he was almost as small as me. Great-grandfather took my hand in both of his.

"Be strong, Kii Yázhí," he rasped, his voice as creaky as an old saddle. I stood up on my toes so that I could put my arms around his neck and then pressed my cheek against his leathery face. "Kii Yázhí," he said again, patting my back. "Our dear little boy."

I had always been small for my age. My father used to tease me about it, saying that when I was born he made my cradleboard out of the handle of a wooden spoon. My baby name was Awéé Yázhí. Little Baby. Little I was and little I stayed. I went from being Awéé Yázhí, Little Baby, to Kii Yázhí, Little Boy.

"You are small," my grandfather said, as if he could hear what I was thinking. "But your heart is large. You will do your best."

I nodded.

When I stepped outside, my mother bent down and embraced me much harder than my grandfather had hugged me. Then she stepped back to stand by the door of our hogan.

6

"Travel safely, my son," Mother said. Her voice was so sad.

My father came up to me and put his broad, calloused hands on my shoulders. He, too, was wearing his best clothing and jewelry. Though he said nothing, I think Father was even sadder than my mother, so sad that words failed him. He was shorter than her, but he was very strong and always stood so straight that he seemed tall as a lodgepole pine to me. His eyes were moist as he lifted me up to the wagon seat and then nodded.

My uncle clucked to the horses and shook the reins. The wagon lurched forward. As I grabbed the wooden backboard to steady myself, I felt a splinter go into my finger from the rough wood, but I ignored the pain. Instead I pulled myself around to turn backward and wave to my parents. I kept waving even after we went around the sagebrush-covered hill and I could no longer see them waving back at me, my father with his back straight and his hand held high, my mother with one hand pressed to her lips while the other floated as gracefully as a butterfly. I did not know it, but it would be quite some time before I saw my home again.

The wheels of the wagon rattled over the ruts in the road. I waved and waved and kept waving. Finally my uncle gently touched me on the wrist. My uncle was the only one in our family who had ever been to the white man's school. His words had helped convince his sister, my mother, to send me to that faraway place. Now he was taking me there, to Gallup, where the mission school was located.

"Kii Yázhí," he said, "look ahead."

I turned to look up at my uncle's kind face. His features were sharp, as hard and craggy as the rocks, but his eyes were friendly and the little mustache he wore softened his mouth. I was frightened by the thought of being away from home for the first time in my life, but I was also trying to find courage. My uncle seemed to know that.

"Little Boy," he said, "Sister's first son, listen to me. You are not going to school for yourself. You are doing this for your family. To learn the ways of the *bilagáanaa*, the white people, is a good thing. Our Navajo language is sacred and beautiful. Yet all the laws of the United States, those laws that we now have to live by, they are in English."

I nodded, trying to understand. It was not easy. Back then, school was such a new thing for our people. My parents and their parents before them had not gone to school to be taught by strangers. They had learned all they knew from their own relatives and from wise elders who knew many things, people who lived with us. People just like us.

My uncle sat quietly for a time, stroking his mustache with the little finger of his right hand. The wagon rattled along, the horses' hooves clopped against the stones in the road. I waited, knowing that my uncle had not yet finished talking. When he stroked his mustache like that, it meant he was thinking and choosing his words with care. It was important not to rush when there was something worthwhile to say.

Then he sighed. "Ah," he said, "your great-grandfather

was your age when the Americans, led by Red Shirt, Kit Carson, made their final war against the Navajos. They wished either to kill us all or remove every Indian from this land. They did this because they did not know us. They did not really understand about the Mexicans."

My uncle turned toward me to see if I understood his words. I politely looked down at my feet and nodded. I knew about the Mexicans. For many years, the Mexicans raided our camps and stole away our people. We were sold as slaves. So our warriors fought back. They raided the villages where our people were held as slaves, rescuing them and taking away livestock from those who attacked us.

"When the Americans came," my uncle continued, "our people tried to be friends with them. But they did not listen to us. They listened to the Mexicans, who could speak their language and said that we were bad people. Instead of helping to free us from slavery, the Americans ordered all the Navajos to stop raiding the slave traders. Some of our bands signed papers and kept the promise not to raid. But each Navajo band had its own headmen. Not all of them signed such papers. So, when all of our people did not stop raiding, the Americans made war on all of the Navajos. They burned our crops, killed our livestock, and cut down our peach trees. They drove our people into exile. They sent us on the Long Walk."

Again my uncle paused to stroke his mustache and again I nodded. I had heard stories about the Long Walk from my great-grandfather. The whole Navajo tribe was forced to walk hundreds of miles to a strange and faraway place the white men called Fort Sumner. Hundreds of our people died along the way and even more died there. The earth was salty and dry. Our corn crops failed year after year. Sometimes late winter storms swept in and men froze while they were trying to work the fields. Our people began to call that place *Hwééldi*, the place where only the wind could live. Our people had no houses, but lived in pits dug into the earth. Indians from other tribes attacked us. We were kept there as prisoners for four winters. Even though I was a little boy, I knew this history as well as my own name.

"Kii Yázhí," my uncle said, his voice slow and serious as he spoke. "It was hard for our people to be so far away from home, but they did not give up. Our people never forgot our homeland between the four sacred mountains. Our people prayed. They did a special ceremony. Then the minds of the white men changed. Our people agreed never again to fight against the United States and they were allowed to go back home. But even though the white men allowed us to come home, we now had to live under their laws. We had to learn their ways. That is why some of us must go to their schools. We must be able to speak to them, tell them who we really are, reassure them that we will always be friends of the United States. That is why you must go to school: not for yourself, but for your family, for our people, for our sacred land."

As my uncle spoke, I saw my great-grandfather's face in my mind. There had been tears of love and pity in his eyes as I left our hogan. I knew now that he had been remembering what it was like when he had been forced to go far away from home. He had been praying life would not be as hard for me at school as it had been for him at Hwééldi.

My uncle dropped his hand onto my shoulder. "Can you do this?" he asked me.

"Yes, Uncle," I said. "I will try hard to learn for our people and our land."

We had reached the hill that marked the edge of our grazing lands. I had never gone beyond that hill before. As my uncle clucked again to the horses, I noticed the pain in my finger and saw the splinter still lodged in it. I carefully worked it free. The tip of that thin needle of wood was red with my blood. Before we went over the hill, I dropped it onto the brown earth. Although I had to go away, I could still leave a little of myself behind.

CHAPTER TWO
Boarding School

The boarding school was more than a hundred miles from my home, so our journey took us several days. We slept out under the silver moon and the bright stars. Each morning my uncle cooked food for us over the fire, usually mutton and beans. Those meals were so good and the time I spent with him was precious to me. I knew I was soon going to be away from all of my family. I shall never forget that journey.

However, what I remember most is the morning of my arrival at Rehoboth Mission. It did not begin well for me. As soon as my uncle reached the gate of the school, like all the other parents and relatives who had traveled far to bring their children there, he was told that he had to go. He patted me one final time on my shoulder, stroked his mustache with his other hand, and nodded slowly.

"You will remember," he said.

He watched me walk through the gate before he climbed back up onto the seat of the wagon, lifted his reins, clucked to the horses, and drove off without looking back. He did not say good-bye. There is no word for good-bye in Navajo.

So I was left standing there, a sad little boy holding tight against my chest the thin blanket in which my few belongings were tied. But I was not alone. There were many other

Navajo children standing there, just as uncertain as I was. Like me, those boys and girls were wearing their finest clothing. Their long black hair glistened from being brushed again and again by loving relatives. The newest deerskin moccasins they owned were on their feet. Like me, many of them wore family jewelry made of silver, inset with turquoise and agate and jet. Our necklaces and bracelets, belts and hair ornaments, were a sign of how much our families loved us, a way of reminding those who would now be caring for us how precious we were in the eyes of our relatives.

Suddenly, as if everyone had remembered their manners all at once, we began to introduce ourselves to each other as Navajos are always supposed to do. We said hello, spoke our names, told each other our clans and where we were from. As you know, our clan system teaches us how we were born and shows us how to grow. By knowing each other's clan—the clan of the mother that we were born to, the clan of the father that we were born for—we can recognize our relatives.

"*Yáát'eeh*," a tall Navajo boy with a red headband said to me. "Hello. I am Many Horses. I am born to Bitter Water Clan and born for Towering House. My birthplace is just west of Chinle below the hills there to the west."

Hearing his polite words made me feel less sad and I answered him slowly and carefully. "*Yáát'eeh*. I am Kii Yázhí. I was born for Mud Clan and Born to Towering House. My birth place is over near Grants. I am the son of Gray Mustache."

A round-faced girl wearing a silky shawl stepped closer

to me and bowed her head. "Hello, my relative," she said. "I am Dawn Girl. I, too, was born to Mud Clan. I am born for Corn Clan."

It was not always easy for me to understand what those other boys and girls were saying. Even though we all spoke in Navajo, we had come from many distant parts of Dinetah. In those days, our language was not spoken the same everywhere by every group of Navajos. But, despite the fact that some of those other children spoke our sacred language differently, what we were doing made me feel happier and more peaceful. We were doing things as our elders had taught us. We were putting ourselves in balance.

Suddenly a huge white man with a red face appeared on the porch above us.

"Be quiet!" he roared at us in English.

Even though most of us could not understand the words he shouted, we all stopped talking. For a moment, before we remembered it is impolite to stare, we all looked up at him. Many of us had seen white people before, when we went to the trading posts with our elders. Almost every trading post was run by white men. Most of them also had their wives and families with them. Because there were no other kids around, those *bilagáanaa* boys and girls often played with the Navajo children. Some of those white traders' children even learned to speak Navajo pretty well—at least much better than their parents.

It is not easy for other people, even other Indians, to learn to speak Navajo properly. The traders always tried to use a little Navajo, but they knew very few words. Sometimes they thought they were saying one thing when they were saying something quite different. I liked to hear the funny way the trader at our post tried to talk Navajo. But I kept a straight face because it would have been rude to laugh at a grown-up, even a grown-up *bilagáanaa* who had just said that all sheep above the age of six should be in school.

However, even though most of us had seen white men before, none of us had ever seen one like that red-faced white man who yelled at us on my first day at the boarding school. His skin was so red that it seemed to be burning. His hair was also that same fiery color. Moreover, his hair was not just on top of his head—where thick hair is supposed to be. It was all over his face. Among Navajos, some men may allow a little hair to grow on their upper lip—just as my uncle and my father did. But this red man had as much hair on his face as an animal. It was on his cheeks, his chin, his neck. Thick red hair even grew out of his ears. He pointed his finger and yelped more words that none of us understood.

"Is that a man speaking or is it a dog?" one of the boys next to me whispered in Navajo.

He wasn't joking. It was a serious question. The huge white man's angry shouts did sound like the barking of a dog. We all put our heads down as that red-dog white man yelped and roared. Finally, he became silent. But he kept staring down at us, waiting for something. When none of us moved, but just stood there, politely looking down at the ground, he barked at us again even louder.

We did not realize that he was ordering us to lift up our faces. We could not understand that he was telling us we must look at him to pay attention. None of us yet had learned that white people expect you to look into their eyes—the way you stare at an enemy when you are about to attack. Among *bilagáanaas,* the only time children look down is when they are ashamed of something.

"What does he want?" a girl whispered in a frightened voice. "He seems angry enough to eat us."

A dark-skinned man with a kind face walked up to stand beside the big, red white man. The red white man growled something at him and the dark-skinned man nodded. Then he turned to us.

"*Yáát'eeh,* my dear children," he said in Navajo in a comforting voice. "My name is Mr. Jacob Benally. I am born to Salt Clan and born for Arrow Clan."

That was when all of us realized this dark-skinned man was Navajo. We had not even thought he was any kind of Indian at all before he spoke. It was not just because he was dressed like a white man, but because his hair was so short. He wore no hat and you could see that all his hair had been cut off close to his scalp. We had never seen a Navajo man with such short hair. Back then, all Navajo men were supposed to have long hair.

Realizing that this man, dressed like a white man, was a Navajo made us look around the school yard. We had already noticed there were many older boys and girls there, all in uniforms. We had thought they were *bilagáanaa* children. They were watching us silently. Now we looked at them differently, seeing that their emotionless faces looked Navajo. But none of them had come to introduce themselves.

Many Horses, the tall boy with the red headband, spoke up.

"My uncle," he said to Mr. Jacob Benally, using the polite form of address to show he respected this man like a relative, "are those other children in *bilagáanaa* clothing also Navajos?"

"Yes, my nephew," Mr. Jacob Benally said, "but I am sorry that I must now tell you something. Listen well. You are forbidden to speak Navajo. You must all speak in English or say nothing at all."

All of us stood there in silence. Most of us did not know any words in English. Those who did know some English words were so shocked that they could not remember any of them. Finally, Mr. Jacob Benally helped us.

"Children," he said in Navajo, "here is a word of greeting that you can say. Watch how I hold my mouth and then repeat it after me. Heh-low. Heh-low."

All of us did as he said. We opened our mouths and made those two sounds. "Heh-low, heh-low, heh-low."

We hoped that this kind Navajo man would stay with us and keep talking Navajo. His job as an interpreter, though, was for one day and one day only. After that he went back to working in the stables and speaking broken English.

The only way left to us was to speak English. Thinking back on it, years later, I see now that it was a good policy in one sense. In the weeks that followed, we learned

English much more quickly because we could not use our native tongue. But I can never forget how sad it made me feel when I learned enough English to understand what the angry, red white man, whose name was Principal O'Sullivan, had to say about our sacred language and our whole Navajo culture.

"Navajo is no good, of no use at all!" Principal O'Sullivan shouted at us every day. "Only English will help you get ahead in this world!"

Although the teachers at the school spoke in quieter tones than our principal, they all said the same. It was no good to speak Navajo or be Navajo. Everything about us that was Indian had to be forgotten.

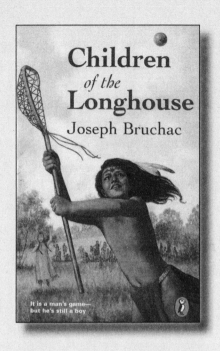

Children
of the
Longhouse

Joseph Bruchac

It is a man's game—
but he's still a boy

When Ohkwa'ri overhears a group of older boys planning a raid on a neighboring village, he immediately tells his Mohawk elders. He has done the right thing—but he has also made enemies. Grabber and his friends will do anything they can to hurt him, especially during the village-wide game of Tekwaarathon (lacrosse). Ohkwa'ri believes in the path of peace, but can peaceful ways work against Grabber's wrath?

"An exciting story that also offers an in-depth look at Native American life centuries ago."   —*Kirkus Reviews*

THE HEART
OF A CHIEF

Can one boy
make a difference?

JOSEPH BRUCHAC

Chris's life is complicated. At school, he's been selected to lead a project on sports teams with Indian names. At home, on the Penacook reservation, the Indians are divided about building a casino. It would destroy the beautiful island Chris thinks of as his own. Is there anything one sixth-grade boy can do?

"Chris's compelling voyage of self-discovery is grounded in everyday events . . . allowing readers to see into the heart of this burgeoning chief."   —*Publishers Weekly*

Joseph Bruchac
Best-selling author of *The Heart of a Chief*

THE
WINTER
PEOPLE

Saxso is fourteen when the British attack his village. It's 1759, and war is raging in the northeast between the British and the French, with the Abenaki people—Saxso's people—by their side. Without enough warriors to defend their homes, Saxso's village is burned to the ground. Many people are killed, but some, including Saxso's mother and two sisters, are taken hostage. Now it's up to Saxso, on his own, to track the raiders and bring his family back home . . . before it's too late.

"Full of history, danger, courage and raw survival."
—*The Dallas Morning News*

WINNER OF THE *DISNEY ADVENTURES* BEST HISTORICAL FICTION AWARD
AN *SLJ* BEST BOOK OF THE YEAR
A NEW YORK PUBLIC LIBRARY BEST BOOK FOR THE TEEN AGE

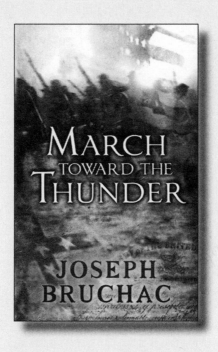

Louis Nolette is not American or Irish; he's an Abenaki Indian from Canada. He's also just fifteen years old. But none of this stops him from joining the Fighting 69th, the Irish Brigade known for its courage and ferocity in battle, during the final years of the Civil War. Louis feels compelled to join up because of the North's commitment to end slavery as well as the promise of good wages. But war is never what you expect, and as he fights in battle after battle, Louis discovers prejudice and acceptance, courage and cowardice in the most unexpected places.

"A fine choice for readers who want war stories that include plenty of action, as well as reflection."   —*Booklist*

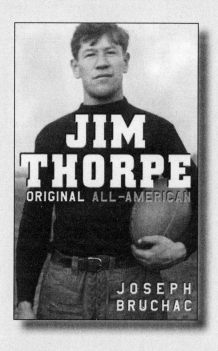

Jim Thorpe was one of the greatest athletes who ever lived. He played professional football and major league baseball, and won Olympic gold medals in track and field. He'll be forever revered by the sports community and by his Native American community. But his life wasn't easy. Born on a reservation, he endured family tragedy and was sent to various Native American boarding schools. Jim ran away from school many times, until he found his calling under the now-legendary coach Pop Warner. This is a book for history buffs as well as sports fans— an illuminating and lively read about a truly great American.

"The novel is a superb blend of fiction and nonfiction, rooted in the author's usual careful research."   —*Kirkus Reviews*